D1555635

HOP-ABOUT

The Adventures of Benny the Bunny and Mr. Rabbit

By Colin Krainin

Illustrations by Joan Platek Krainin

Copyright © 2020 Colin Krainin
All rights reserved.

Published by Crowell Creek Books.

Book Cover Design by ebooklaunch.com

Original Cover Drawing by Joan Platek Krainin

Illustrations by Joan Platek Krainin

For Sas and The Gal

TABLE OF CONTENTS

MR. RABBIT

Mr. Rabbit certainly did not like to brag, but he couldn't help but be aware that he was a rather handsome stuffed rabbit. His fur was a light, soft grey with just a hint of brown. His ears were lovingly floppy and generously sized. His body was slim and pear-shaped, his arms straight and long. A particular point of pride was his pink nose that sat at the point of his rounded snout. It was heart-shaped and gave him a touch of pizzazz, if he didn't say so himself. The nose was positioned close to a small pursed mouth and two small black eyes that shone with curiosity and a rather congenial manner.

If Mr. Rabbit were to be completely honest, he would have to admit that his feet were the source of no small amount of joy. They were very large—in fact, larger than the legs that attached them to his pear-shaped torso. Not only did they look bold and charming, they were also very practical, allowing him to hop great distances—a particular advantage when you were only a seven-inch-tall stuffed rabbit. They were also quite ticklish, although he didn't like to spread that information around too far in case some miscreant might take advantage. But the sensitivity was also nice, and he often found himself enjoying rubbing them together or running them along little folds in the sheets of his bed when he got sleepy. Oh yes, and the summer grass felt delightful as he hopped along, with the stiff blades of grass providing little twitches of pleasure with each hop.

If you watched Mr. Rabbit hopping through the grass in Central Park or wherever you might find him, he'd probably bring a smile to your lips. After all, he was quite a handsome stuffed rabbit and very gentle and nice. And very curious about the world too. You might see him having hopped up on a bed of flowers, bent over into the petals of a rose, sniffing its smell, his white puff of a tail twitching in rhythm to the twitches of his pink nose while it smelled a delightful smell, not quite the same as any he'd smelled before.

When Mr. Rabbit would discover something new, he'd concentrate very hard to make sure he could distinguish all that made it unique. He'd think about the rose smell, "Mmmmm, I think it smells a bit sharp. Like it's poking you a bit. But also kind of misty, like it wants to wrap you up in a blanket of warm, wet air. And definitely a bit like you might imagine a beautiful dress would smell if it were woven by angels. And just a hint of dirt too. Like a dash of freshly tilled morning dirt."

And having discovered such a splendid new thing, Mr. Rabbit would almost certainly want to go tell his best friend Benny the Bunny about it. Sniffing that delightful rose smell, Mr. Rabbit thought to himself, "Ho ha, I bet Benny the Bunny would love this." And so he started hopping home so he could tell Benny the Bunny all about it.

Mr. Rabbit lived in Apartment 1K in a fifteen-story building in the Upper West Side of New York City with Benny the Bunny and his other friend, Dr. Ursa, who was a large stuffed brown bear. Dr. Ursa was very nice to hug because he would envelop Mr. Rabbit with his big bear arms and Mr. Rabbit would just about sink into his soft bear fur. Dr. Ursa was very smart. He had to be in order to be a wawatrician, which meant that he was a doctor that took care of stuffed animals or, as they are more formally known, wawas. Dr. Ursa wouldn't be at home yet when Mr. Rabbit got back from Central Park because he would still be at his office taking care of his patients' various ailments: a bit of fluff coming out where it shouldn't, or an eye that had been jostled, or perhaps just a case of the sniffles.

As Mr. Rabbit hopped along home, he thought about how Dr. Ursa was not only very smart but also an exceptional cook. Mr. Rabbit sighed a bit and smacked his lips, thinking about Dr. Ursa standing over the stove in the kitchen, with his green cooking apron covered in beautiful birds of all different types, cooking up some nice root vegetables for Mr. Rabbit and Benny the Bunny to eat.

When Mr. Rabbit got back to his building, Pedro the doorman was there to greet him. Pedro was an excellent doorman and a wonderful person. Just as Mr. Rabbit got back to the building, two schoolchildren, Jane and Sara, were entering the doorway before him. They both called out, "Hey, Pedro!" And Pedro's dazzling smile spread out over his face. "Hey! Hey!" he called. "How was school today?"

"Goooood," they both said, drawing out the sound of the word. Then, as was tradition, they both gave Pedro high-fives as they went inside the building toward their elevator.

"Hey, Mr. Rabbit," called Pedro as he saw Mr. Rabbit hopping in the entrance of the building.

"Hey, Pedro," Mr. Rabbit called out, then he too hopped up (quite a distance, mind you) to give Pedro a high-five.

"Hey! Hey!" said Pedro, always excited to get a good high-five and to see Mr. Rabbit. "What's the story today? What's new?"

"Well," said Mr. Rabbit, "I just smelled a very excellent new smell in the park and was heading in to tell Benny the Bunny all about it."

"OK!" said Pedro with enthusiasm. "I like myself a good smell as well. And a good day to be out in the park too."

"That's right!" said Mr. Rabbit, matching Pedro's enthusiasm. "The park was just like ..." Mr. Rabbit let out a deeply satisfied sigh, "really wonderful today."

Pedro had a small station to sit at right where one entered the southern entrance of the building. Except for Apartment 1K, all the apartments required that you walk past Pedro into the interior of the building and take an elevator. But Apartment 1K was special. The entrance was directly across from where Pedro sat, right there at the entrance to the building.

Apartment 1K had a human-sized door, but its stuffed rabbit residents had figured out a system to easily open it when they were on their own. They would hop up onto the radiator next to their door, then hop over onto the door knob, dangle a bit and insert the key, and—open sesame—they rode the swinging door inside, hopped onto the stair bannister, then down onto the third step. Dr. Ursa was significantly larger, and he could reach the key into the keyhole by standing on his tippy toes and stretching his body out as far as it went. But most of the time, like today, Pedro was right there to open the door for whichever stuffed animal needed to get inside.

Pedro tipped his hat and closed the door behind Mr. Rabbit as he thanked Pedro for letting him in. After entering the front door to Apartment 1K, a person or a stuffed animal found themselves in a small vestibule. There were two big closets to hang coats in, which the stuffed animals had divided into a human-sized portion and beneath that, a stuffed animal–sized portion. There were also some small cubbies where the stuffed animals could keep their shoes and boots and galoshes. Mostly the rabbits eschewed wearing footwear whenever possible, but in the winter they liked to make sure their lower paws were warm and didn't get patches of snow and ice stuck to their fur. Also, you never knew when you might have a formal occasion where you needed to slip on some evening slippers in order to maintain propriety. In between the two big closets was a covered radiator that someone might sit upon while they put their boots on or took them off. When the radiator was on in the winter, the area on top would become quite toasty, and it felt very nice on Mr. Rabbit's backside to sit there and warm up after a long day hopping out in the snow.

When entering the vestibule from the front door, immediately to the right was a set of stairs and a bannister. Mr. Rabbit hopped up those stairs toward the built-in bookshelf at the top. Here Benny the Bunny kept a portion of his library of books, specifically his more technical nonfiction volumes (his fiction and histories being kept in the library proper in the second bedroom). Because the bookshelf reached up so high, Benny the Bunny had a ladder set against it so that he could climb to just the shelf he wanted and get the exact book he desired to read at that moment.

Hopping all the way to the top of the stairs, Mr. Rabbit turned left, went through the open French doors, and into the living room. Apartment 1K wasn't particularly large by human standards, but for three stuffed animals, it was very luxurious. The living room, kitchen, one bathroom, and master bedroom were laid out so as to accommodate both humans and stuffed rabbits (or any other creatures that might like to visit, like cuddly dogs or soft-furred cats or any of the wild rabbits or groundhogs that Mr. Rabbit counted amongst his friends). The ceilings in this portion were fifteen feet high, which was high even for humans. In the master bedroom, Benny the Bunny, Mr. Rabbit, and Dr. Ursa had three perfectly sized little beds to sleep in, as well as a Japanese silk screen with beautiful trees and flowers on it that divided the room. On the other side of the silk screen was a human-sized twin bed, in case they had an overnight human visitor, and a very fluffy tan dog bed in case they had an animal visitor that preferred to be closer to the ground.

Mr. Rabbit hopped along through the living room and kitchen and master bedroom looking for Benny the Bunny, but he couldn't find him. He must be in the second bedroom, he thought, and hopped along the hall that separated the living room from the two bedrooms.

The wawas called the area one entered going through the four-foot-tall door past the master bedroom the *second bedroom*, but only because that was what it was called when humans had lived in Apartment 1K. While the rest of Apartment 1K was laid out so as to be accessible to all visitors, in the second bedroom, the wawas had taken advantage of their small stature in designing the layout. What had been a second bedroom with a fifteen-foot-high ceiling was now four floors of rooms.

The first floor contained all the conveniences of modern stuffed animal life. There was a music room, an art and crafts room, and a padded yoga/exercise/dance room. There was even a sauna room for Dr. Ursa (and occasionally Benny the Bunny and Mr. Rabbit) to have a schvitz. The second floor was made up of each of the stuffed animals' offices. Mr. Rabbit had his art studio, Benny the Bunny his writer's studio, and Dr. Ursa his home office full of plastic models of various types of stuffed animal bodies. (Dr. Ursa's office was the smallest because he primarily worked out of his private medical practice office situated at the northern end of the building.) The third and fourth floors made up a large wood-paneled library. The third floor was a full floor, but there was a large square hole in the middle of the fourth floor so that a great dazzling chandelier could hang and illuminate both floors. It was there on the third floor, sitting at a large table reading a leather-bound, rabbit-sized copy of *Moby-Dick* that Mr. Rabbit found Benny the Bunny.

Seeing Benny the Bunny's fiercely concentrated reading face caused an enormous smile to stretch across Mr. Rabbit's little mouth. Like Mr. Rabbit, Benny the Bunny was a partly human-shaped stuffed rabbit, but he had longer legs and smaller feet. From his feet to the top of his head, he was about twelve inches tall. But while Mr. Rabbit was a floppy-eared rabbit, Benny the Bunny's ears stuck straight up, adding another three and a half inches to his apparent height. He was almost entirely light brown in color, except he had a white-grey muzzle around his mouth as well as white-grey circles around beautiful black eyes that were set a bit to the side, so that he could see well to the sides and even almost behind him.

Mr. Rabbit loved Benny the Bunny with all of his heart. So much so that just thinking about it brought a bit of water to Mr. Rabbit's eyes and a funny heaving looseness to his whole chest area. Benny the Bunny, Mr. Rabbit reflected, was a very intelligent rabbit, but more than intelligent, he was wise. Always knowing not just the proper thing to do but also the right, kindest thing to do.

As Mr. Rabbit hopped up to his seat, Benny the Bunny looked up suddenly from reading his book, slightly startled to find Mr. Rabbit so close.

"Hi ho, Benny!" called Mr. Rabbit, giving the older rabbit a bit of a squeeze.

"Oh, Mr. Rabbit. How are you? Have you been enjoying the park?" asked Benny the Bunny, turning to return Mr. Rabbit's hug.

"Oh, so very much. I smelled a very lovely smell I hadn't smelled before," Mr. Rabbit said.

"That's wonderful. Could you tell me about it?" asked Benny the Bunny.

"Absolutely!" said Mr. Rabbit. And Mr. Rabbit proceeded to tell Benny the Bunny all about the rose smell he had smelled in Central Park in great detail.

When he was done, Benny the Bunny said, "Well, that sounds just perfectly lovely. Say, I think The Natural Store sells freshly cut roses out front. What do you say we hop over to The Natural Store and buy some roses and put them in a vase so that we can smell them in the living room and so that Dr. Ursa can smell them too when he gets home?"

"That's a great idea!" replied Mr. Rabbit, and so it was decided.

***

A few minutes later, once Benny the Bunny had put his book away and got himself sorted, Mr. Rabbit found himself back outside on the sidewalk bounding along next to the taller rabbit, heading a few blocks uptown toward The Natural Store.

One of the daily difficulties of being a stuffed rabbit in New York City was that there was often quite a bit of foot traffic, which led to lots of rapidly swung human shoes and legs. So Mr. Rabbit and Benny the Bunny had learned to be very careful and weave in and out of the crowds in order to avoid any collisions. Sometimes they would exchange knowing nods and raised eyebrows with smaller dogs that also had to navigate a maze of distracted and briskly walking humans.

The Natural Store had lots of excellent items for stuffed rabbits: fresh vegetables and fruits, grains, a whole aisle of teas and coffee, and sweet treats to eat along with a hot cup of coffee or tea. Today, however, the rabbits did not go inside The Natural Store, but instead Benny the Bunny took Mr. Rabbit to a display on the outside wall of the store. The whole wall was bursting with all sorts of flowers. Mr. Rabbit couldn't believe it! He stood there stock-still with his little pursed mouth falling slightly open.

"Ho ha, Benny!" he exclaimed. "Would you look at all those flowers!"

There were daffodils and tulips and lilacs and oh so many roses! There were pink roses and red roses and yellow-orange roses and even white roses.

"You should give them all a smell, Mr. Rabbit," replied Benny the Bunny.

So Mr. Rabbit hopped up onto the boxes that held the flowers to the wall. He stuck his little pink nose into the petals of a lilac and took a big inhale. "Oh my!" he called. Then he hopped over onto another box, this one containing the pink roses, and gave another sniff. "I say!" he called. He kept it up, smelling all the different fresh cut flowers along the wall. Finally, he hopped back down to where Benny the Bunny stood.

"Wow!" Mr. Rabbit said. "That was, like, really, really great. So many beautifully smelling flowers. The roses didn't smell quite as nice as the ones in the wild, but there were so many different types of smells to pick from, it was just so wonderful."

"What color roses do you think we should buy?" asked Benny the Bunny.

"Um, well, I like them all," said Mr. Rabbit. "Maybe you should get to pick, Benny, since you had the very excellent idea to come here."

So Benny the Bunny picked out a dozen yellow-orange roses. He thought they were very warm and friendly looking and would be just the thing to brighten their living room. Having paid for the roses, the rabbits started to hop their way home, each rabbit holding six yellow-orange roses each. As they turned the corner to the entrance to their building, one of their favorite neighbors, a very kind older gentleman named John, was leaving to go on a walk with two of their favorite dogs in the world, Malcolm and Tuck. Malcolm was a robust golden-colored Cairn Terrier and Tuck was a slender dark-colored Cairn Terrier with streaks of lighter golden color in his fur. Sometimes Tuck's combination fur looked almost silver in the right light.

John waved to the two rabbits and Malcolm and Tuck became very excited to see them, and the roses as well, because they yanked as hard as they could against their leashes and ran up to the rabbits, calling, "Ruff! Ruff!" Malcolm was so excited to see Benny the Bunny, he gave him a big friendly lick, while Tuck nuzzled Mr. Rabbit with his nose.

"Hey there, fellas," called Mr. Rabbit, a big smile coming to his face. "Here, smell these roses. They smell really terrific." Mr. Rabbit lowered his bundle of roses in the direction of Malcolm and Tuck, who aggressively stuck their noses in the bundle and took big whopping sniffs. The smell was indeed so terrific that the two dogs bounded about in glee, a good smell being even more delicious for a dog than for a stuffed rabbit.

The rabbits said their hellos and goodbyes to John and the two dogs, making sure to give them friendly pats on their fur, then they hopped back inside. Pedro was once again at the entrance to the building.

"Hi ho, Pedro!" Mr. Rabbit called to him. "Remember earlier when I smelled that really good rose smell? Well, I went and bought some fresh cut ones with Benny the Bunny. We got you one because you said you loved really great smells." And Mr. Rabbit handed the most perfect of the yellow-orange roses to Pedro.

Pedro took a big sniff of the rose. "It's wonderful!" he said, a bit of mist coming to his eyes. "I'll tell you what. I'm going to keep this with me all day so I have something nice to smell. Then, when I'm ready to go home, I'll cut the bloom off the stem and pin it to my coat lapel so I can wear it and look very handsome on my way home and for my wife and kids. Then tonight I'll press it into a notebook to preserve it."

"That's a great idea!" said both the rabbits, smiling. So Pedro let them back into Apartment 1K, where they went about putting the roses in a vase so that there would be a wonderful little touch of joy for Dr. Ursa when he came home from his long day of work.

And indeed it was. Dr. Ursa was a bit slumped and worn out when he first came into the apartment. Even his fur looked a bit droopy. There had been too many patients and too little time today. But when he saw the flowers in a vase on the side table just past the French doors, a big bear smile lit his face, and he pressed his nose deep into the bouquet and took a big bear huff and sighed a big bear sigh of satisfaction.

Hearing Dr. Ursa come in, the rabbits bounded into the living room with excitement and gave Dr. Ursa welcoming hugs. Then they helped him cook some root vegetables up in the kitchen, just the smell of which pleased Mr. Rabbit to no end, all the while chit-chatting about their days—about all the patients, and reading *Moby-Dick*, and smelling the roses in Central Park, as the case may be. Then they sat together and ate their dinner (Dr. Ursa had snuck a little salmon in the oven for himself as well), each one periodically glancing over at the roses that added a splash of color to the room and an ethereal sense of peace as well.

And as they ate and chatted, Benny the Bunny began to feel full and rather comfortable. And with his feeling of comfort came the subtler, harder-to-fathom feeling of nostalgia. Old images and old times played across his mind. Almost as if they had a will of their own, he found himself talking of those old stories from what almost felt like a different life. Back when he had lived in an old house in Massachusetts with woods out back that seemed to go on and on forever.

Feeling very nostalgic indeed, Benny the Bunny began to tell Mr. Rabbit stories that mostly revolved around his old childhood friend, the shockingly orange and bountifully bombastic wawa, Custerd the cat. Most of the stories were comedies—light and funny. But some were tragedies—like the mysterious disappearance of the other wawa in the group, Rogo the lion.

A very few of the stories were an unpredictable mixture of both comedy and tragedy, and those were the tales that Mr. Rabbit found himself turning over in his head as he went to sleep that night. How even in happy moments, they were marked about the edges with shadows of melancholy. But shining through the melancholy there often came, as sudden as the first aching sprouts of spring, a kind of grace.

Mr. Rabbit listened to Benny the Bunny weave his tales with rapt attention, not wanting to miss a single word. Never guessing that Custerd would soon change his life forever.

THE DOG PARK

On Sunday afternoons Benny and Mr. Rabbit go to their favorite dog park to watch the dogs play. They usually leave for the park in the mid-afternoon once their lunches are fully digested and they start to feel a bit tired. A walk to the dog park can be just the thing to perk them up for the rest of the day.

This afternoon, after giving a big wave and a hearty "How do you do?" to Pedro, they strolled down the sidewalk toward Riverside Park, where the best dog park in the city resided. The day was sunny and cool. Autumn had fully set in. Mr. Rabbit enjoyed the crispness in the air and the scent of falling leaves all around. As he hopped along, he really did begin to perk up, thinking how lucky he was to be able to spend an afternoon watching all sorts of dogs play.

When they crossed West End Avenue, Benny made sure they looked both ways even though the walk sign was on. Benny was very cautious and very wise. As they hopped along, he continued to look in both directions, enjoying the view of all the old beautiful buildings that lined West End Avenue. Benny loved his apartment, but he imagined it would be very nice to live in one of these buildings as well. He could just see Pedro opening the door for them into one of those old grand entryways. He imagined the sparkling chandeliers and the marbled floors. And there would be a nice comfortable desk for Pedro to sit at when he was making sure everyone was safe and that all the residents knew that he was happy to see them. Maybe someday Benny would make a friend in one of those buildings and he could come over to visit and see what it was like. And then maybe that friend could come to his building and meet Pedro and Dr. Ursa and Mr. Rabbit. Maybe they could all have some lovely tea together. Snack on some special turnips. But not too many. Easy did it with turnips.

They entered Riverside Park at 97th Street. Children were playing on the swings there. The rabbits saw Mrs. Carmichael, who lived on the third floor of their building, pushing her daughter Jane on the swings. Benny and Mr. Rabbit waved at Mrs. Carmichael and Jane. Mr. Rabbit called out, "Um, hello, Mrs. Carmichael; hello, Jane. Lovely day in the park, isn't it?" When Mrs. Carmichael and Jane saw the two rabbits, they yelled back their greetings, and both had big smiles on their faces because it was indeed lovely to see such gentlemanly rabbits heading out for some time in the park.

"Whatcha ya up to today, boys?" Mrs. Carmichael yelled up to the rabbits.

"Just headin' over to the old dog park," said Mr. Rabbit.

"Isn't it wonderful?" asked Mrs. Carmichael, but she really meant it as a statement.

"Oh yes," answered Mr. Rabbit, and a little smile came to his pursed mouth in anticipation of seeing all the fluffy dogs there.

"Well, have a time, boys. We've got to enjoy these days while we got 'em," yelled Mrs. Carmichael. The rabbits gave a last wave and started to hop their way into the park proper.

Riverside Park was wonderful any time of year, but in the spring and in the autumn it was extraordinary. All the trees were fully covered in beautifully colored leaves—red and gold and orange, and many leaves that were still green too. Mr. Rabbit thought about how lucky he was to live so close to such a beautiful park.

"Don't you think that Riverside Park is wonderful all the time, Benny, but that in the spring and autumn, it's especially wonderful?" Mr. Rabbit asked.

Benny was quiet a moment as he thought about the question. That was one of Benny's strong suits. He didn't say anything before he gave a good little think to make sure he said exactly what he meant.

"I do," agreed Benny. "But I also think all of New York City is especially wonderful in the spring and the autumn. The winter can sometimes be a little cold and dark. And that can be nice when you curl up inside, but sometimes you have to go out, and the cold can get through your fur and into your bones and make you want to go back inside and have some hot cocoa. The summer is special too. Lots of time to hop in the park and play games in the grass. Sometimes the days seem to last forever and you feel full of life. But other times it gets a bit too hot, and when you have a lot of fur like we do, one gets a bit run down out on the city streets. So you want to come in and drink some cold water with maybe a few fruits floating in it to nibble on. And sometimes you think that it would be nice to head out to the country and flop in a river or lake."

"That's just what I was thinking," said Mr. Rabbit.

"Let me ask you something," said Benny. "If you were absolutely forced to pick, which season do you like best, the autumn or the spring?"

By the time Benny asked that question, the rabbits had just about hopped their way to the dog park. Mr. Rabbit could already see the bustle and hustle and flashes of fur of the dogs as they raced and jumped around in great explosions of excitement.

"Hmmm," said Mr. Rabbit, thinking over the question. He wanted to follow Benny's example of thinking over questions carefully, so he worked the question around in his mind for a good few moments. But it felt like a very big question, and he found himself answering before he could fully work out all the details.

"I suppose, if I absolutely had to pick, that I would pick the autumn. The spring's all bursting with flowers and that special little buzzing feeling of having been through the winter, but now the sun's out and everyone's very grateful. Lots of great smells and beautiful colors. But there's, mmmmm, *something* about the autumn. Like in the spring, the flowers are just *so* beautiful. But the flowers are very special things and they grow in special places. In the autumn, all the leaves everywhere turn different colors. They are already beautiful when they're green, but when they are also red and orange and yellow, it's like every leaf's a flower, and I'm like, 'Wow! Look at that.' And they're like, 'Hey Mr. Rabbit, remember, you don't have to be a special thing growing in a special place to be special.' And I don't know. I think it's hard to say just what I mean. Right now, walking in the park with all the different-colored leaves, I guess it makes me feel that feeling like— you know how it's nice when you're with one of your friends, but sometimes you get to be with just about all of your friends at the same time. And you feel like you just fit right in there and you don't even have to say or do anything to just *fit* perfectly. I think the autumn makes me feel like that—like I'm with all of my friends."

As Mr. Rabbit finished his explanation, the two stuffed rabbits had made it all the way to the dog park and were just hopping up onto one of the wooden benches located within the fenced-in area of the dog park. They settled themselves down, their rabbit feet dangling in the air over the side of the bench, and began to take in the full spectacle of the dogs playing before them.

There were many excellent dogs in the park. Some were big and noble and handsome. Some were small and fluffy and cute. Some looked very clever. And some looked very silly. Some of them liked to run around and around, while others liked to roll on their backs. Some of the dogs were in a big scrum, rearing up on their front legs and playfully dropping their paws against one another. Malcolm and Tuck were there, chasing a ball that John threw out to them, and then whoever got to it first would bring it back to where John was seated on a bench on the other side of the dog park from the rabbits.

The rabbits sat quietly there a while, just drinking in all the festivities, their hearts warmed by the unconscious play of the dogs. That is, until a furry bumblebee buzzed its way over to Mr. Rabbit and landed gently on his shoulder.

At first Mr. Rabbit ignored the light tickling feeling, thinking it was just one of those random tickles one felt for no particular reason from time to time. But after a few moments he became suspicious because the tickle seemed to move about strangely, almost like something was walking on him, so he turned his head only to find himself eyeball to compound eyeball with a big furry bumblebee.

Mr. Rabbit knew that he should not overreact to a (most likely) very kindly bumblebee that just wanted to find a pretty flower to pollinate, but he was rather startled by the bumblebee's so sudden appearance. And for Mr. Rabbit, being only a seven-inch-tall stuffed rabbit, a large bumblebee was no small insect.

"Ahhhh!" called Mr. Rabbit in fright once the presence of the bumblebee was processed by the primordial part of his brain. He popped up to standing on the bench and twisted about from side to side, swatting all about his head with his paws. Yet all this seemed to accomplish was to send the bumblebee into a buzzing harrumph. He flew in rapid little circles around Mr. Rabbit's head, darting in and out, landing briefly on a flopping ear or pink nose and generally disorienting the poor rabbit.

Then a rather unfortunate thing happened.

In his disorientation, Mr. Rabbit took a false step right off the bench, out into the empty air, and then smack onto the snoozing back of a black Labrador retriever mix whose name turned out to be Felix. Now Felix was in his prime retrieving years and in tippy-top running shape. Until Mr. Rabbit landed squarely on his back and the bumblebee landed with a loud buzz right between his eyes, Felix had been dreaming of running after a tennis ball that never slowed down but was endlessly racing out in front of him.

Between his already-running sleeping mind and the shock of being awakened by a falling Mr. Rabbit and buzzing bumblebee, Felix acted on pure instinct and took off like a shot to escape whatever assault was upon him. It was all that Mr. Rabbit could do to hang on to Felix's back fur for dear life (and similarly for the bumblebee, who desperately clung to Felix's snout).

When the bumblebee had first arrived on Mr. Rabbit's shoulder, Benny the Bunny had been lost in a kind of contemplative stupor as he stared out over the playing dogs. If you were to tap him on the shoulder and say, "Hey, whatcha thinking about right now?" he could only smile, shake his head, and say, "Well, I don't really know. But I know my mind must be working on some problem below the level of consciousness so that later today I might, say, sit down to work on the mystery novel I've been writing, and then boom, some problem with constructing the plot completely falls away and I know just what to do."

Being in this kind of distant, out-of-body contemplative state, Benny the Bunny did not notice that Mr. Rabbit was in a tussle with a bumblebee until hearing the commotion as he fell onto Felix's back. "Oh no!" thought Benny as he watched Felix race away, Mr. Rabbit riding on his back, his paws clutching Felix's soft black fur. "Oh no!" thought Benny again. Then he hopped off the bench and began to hop after the sprinting Felix.

First, Felix took a big, faster-than-thought circle around the dog park. Mr. Rabbit thought "Ooooooooooo!" as he held on best he could. As Felix raced about, Tuck, John's dark-haired Cairn Terrier, noticed what was happening. Tuck was quite an intelligent young dog. He stopped his ball-playing and called to Malcolm, the golden-haired Cairn Terrier, and said, "Ruff! … ruff!" Malcolm looked at Tuck, who

16

rapidly jerked his head toward the unfolding scene. Malcolm then turned to see Felix running like a crazed maniac with Mr. Rabbit on top of him, head and paws buried in his fur and Benny the Bunny hopping after them.

"Ruff! Rrruff!" called Tuck, and Malcolm understood. Tuck was a very intelligent young Cairn Terrier, but he deferred to the more heavily muscled Malcolm in feats of strength and speed. Malcolm gave Tuck a quick nod and took off after Felix and the two rabbits.

After having looped around its fenced-in area, Felix bolted through the dog park gate just as a dog walker with six Yorkshire Terriers with leashes all tangled up was attempting to enter through the gate. It was at this moment that Benny the Bunny saw Malcolm chasing after him. "Ruff! Ruff!" Malcolm called as he caught up with Benny the Bunny— no further words being necessary.

Benny the Bunny hopped and swung himself up onto Malcolm's back, and the two of them raced out of the gate and past the same befuddled dog walker into Riverside Park proper.

Malcolm ran at full gallop. Two paws reached out long together, then Benny felt the light grace of impact, thrusting him briefly forward, then the explosion of the two rear paws and he was pressed back and flat against Malcolm's back. Benny held his head slightly up in the racing wind to keep the blur of black that was Felix in his sights. Meanwhile, they flung past the people milling about Riverside Park, their speed making the people seem like statues. The regularly spaced trees that lined the path pulsed in Benny's vision like a beat. A beat that Malcolm made more rapid with each arching galloping thrust of his body.

Speed. More speed. Impossibly more speed. The black blur grew larger. While Felix's eyes were wide and he ran with the speed of fear, Malcolm's eyes were utterly blank and he ran without force or purpose. There was no thought. No emotion. There was only the essential truth of his being. Love of speed. Love of the chase. Every molecule in his body cried out for it. Made speed into his monument. His offering. Made holy the act of speed.

The golden blur drew up to the black blur. Up to Felix's hindquarters. And not a second too soon. Felix was fast approaching a big wet patch of mud at the end of the tree-lined passage they'd been racing down.

And with one more powerful leaping stride, Malcolm drew parallel to Felix. Benny drew himself up, prepared for his moment. The impact of the stride finding earth. The contraction of the muscle beneath him. The floating freedom of the air as Malcolm leaped forward again. And at the crescendo of the stride, Benny himself leaped into the air, sideways and forward.

For a moment, all was floating and falling and no tether to the sanity of the ground. Then—POW! Benny landed on Felix's back, just in front of Mr. Rabbit. There was a close-run instant when Benny feared he would not be able to hold his momentum from taking him right over the other side of Felix and crashing to the ground. But he was able to bury a paw firmly in the black fur and just barely hold on.

Benny pressed his head forward. Brought his mouth up to Felix's ear. "It's OK now. It's OK. There's no need to fear." To Felix it was like the words came from within his own mind. And for the first moment since he'd begun his frenzied run, a rational thought entered his mind.

And that thought was "mud."

Felix hit the brakes hard. There was a momentary skid and a sudden stop. Barely—just barely—he managed to avoid the mud, stopping precisely at its edge.

Meanwhile, momentum and the sudden stop threw Mr. Rabbit and Benny the Bunny right off Felix's back on two parallel arcs, up for a floating moment, then down, plop, straight into the wet mud.

When John and Tuck arrived a moment later with Felix's younger but far less in-shape owner trailing well behind him, they were greeted with the following sight: Felix and Malcolm, fast becoming friends, dancing about together at the edge of the mud patch, and two rather disheveled but always dignified rabbits lying on their backs in the brown mud. The precipitating bumblebee was nowhere to be found.

Seeing John and Malcolm, Mr. Rabbit called out, "Oh, say, John, sorry for the commotion. A big furry bumblebee, you know. Out of nowhere, and now gone. Back to ... nowhere, I guess. Um, anyways. Well, would anyone have a hand or a paw to help us out? We're a bit stuck in the mud, so to speak."

***

18

The tub in the bathroom in Apartment 1K was built for humans, so there was plenty of space for two rabbits to float in a bubble bath and recover from the day's events.

John had, of course, helped them out of the mud patch. And then they had all walked home together. Despite being all muddy, Mr. Rabbit very much enjoyed chatting with John and patting Malcolm and Tuck. Both rabbits thanked the dogs profusely for their timely assistance—Tuck for his great idea and Malcolm for his heroic athleticism.

Now, slowly drifting along the surface of the bath, his fur all covered in bubbles, Mr. Rabbit let his mind wander and recall his rather eventful Sunday afternoon.

"Benny?" he asked, not picking his head up but just calling upward, his head relaxed backward in its floating position.

"Yes?" Benny the Bunny called upward as well, also not moving his head from its floating position, not wanting to break the deep relaxation that only seems possible after a significant exertion. Total relaxation like this for Benny the Bunny was a true rarity. Even his ears were relaxed as they floated amongst the bubbles.

"Thanks for coming to my rescue."

"Of course, Mr. Rabbit. No need to thank me."

A moment passed.

"Benny?"

"Yes?"

"Want to know something maybe a little bad?"

"OK," said Benny the Benny. "You can tell me anything."

"When I was holding on to Felix and he was running really fast … it was scary, but … it was also … *fun*. I know I shouldn't have been having fun. But it was really, really fun."

Benny paused a moment. Then a smile stretched across his little mouth.

"It *was* fun, wasn't it?" agreed Benny.

And both rabbits, as relaxed as can be, floated there, covered in bubbles, little smiles on their faces as they remembered the dog park.

BENNY THE BUNNY NO. 17

In their own way, each of the wawas in Apartment 1K was a creature of habit. On weekdays, Dr. Ursa's alarm would wake everyone up at precisely 6:17 a.m. The instant of the alarm's first piercing call would be punctuated by the sound of Dr. Ursa's paw smashing onto his alarm clock, followed inevitably by a long bear groan. At this series of noises, Benny's eyes would snap open, the rest of his brown rabbit body remaining perfectly still, as if his brain had sprung awake but his muscles had decided to hit the snooze button.

Mr. Rabbit didn't have to hit the snooze button but had pre-programmed his alarm to sound at 6:32 a.m. While Dr. Ursa inexplicably chose to have a classic chirping alarm, Mr. Rabbit's alarm was a rotation of classical music pieces—Bach, Mozart, Beethoven, and especially Chopin's nocturnes—that lightly massaged the small rabbit's brain from sleep to alertness. So when Dr. Ursa's alarm briefly sounded, this was merely the signal for Mr. Rabbit to roll from sleeping on one side to the other, rub his feet together, and smack his lips a bit as his brain cycled through memories of the night's many pleasant dreams.

First thing in the morning was exercise time. After the incident in the dog park, Benny the Bunny had taken up jogging. The incident had revealed to him that his youthful speed had somewhat deteriorated over perhaps too many comfortable days of enjoying warm cocoa, coffees and teas, a nibble or two of a scone now and then, putting his feet up and losing himself in a good book, or just sitting on a Riverside Park bench with Mr. Rabbit and watching the sun set over New Jersey. Now, Benny knew that all of these things were amongst the most excellent things in life, but one must also make time to take care of the physical as well. And while Malcolm had come to the rescue one time, Benny knew it was unwise to rely on outside forces, and that he himself should be prepared to do the running if necessary.

By the late fall, Benny had for some time been in a regular jogging routine. After his eyes snapped open from Dr. Ursa's alarm, he would allow the forces within him to debate between the merits of doing what he ought to and just sleeping a bit longer this *one* time. Once he let those forces have their little ritualistic argument, he would just start moving, ignoring the argument altogether. While the mind might be a few steps behind in the morning, the body respected action and movement, not endless deliberation.

So while Dr. Ursa huffed himself off his bed and began to bang about making the coffee and some other initial breakfast preparations, Benny would slip on some sweats, it being more than a bit nippy at this point in the fall, and head out of the door, giving a hearty but still groggy morning wave to Pedro (who was miraculously already at work at this early hour) as he began to less and less stiffly and more and more joyfully warm up from a fast walk, to a slow jog, to a real run, to an almost effortless glide down the sidewalks to Riverside Park, where morning after morning he would see the same familiar faces running or walking in the opposite direction (and a few new ones giving it a shot too). Seeing those faces, both old and new, made Benny feel like he was part of something bigger than himself, part of the great churn of the city, its living vibration that called out "Look upon my buildings and parks and endless drama, my relentless work and my grand ambitions; go just a little further beyond yourself. Meet me halfway and we all shall be lifted up together."

Feeling these things, Benny's heart would warm and a smile would perk along the edges of his mouth. It was wonderful to feel a part of the city.

When Benny would be just about approaching the midpoint of his jog, Mr. Rabbit would have finally gotten out of bed and made his way to the living room to meet Dr. Ursa just having finished up his breakfast preparations. Mr. Rabbit and Dr. Ursa preferred exercise of the indoor variety and stuck rigorously to a five-day rotation: tai chi on Mondays, yoga on Tuesdays, Wednesday was Pilates day, Thursday old-fashioned calisthenics, and Friday was, of course, classical stretch day.

The timing usually worked out fairly well, so that by the time Benny was back from his jog and finishing up his post-run stretches, Mr. Rabbit and Dr. Ursa were finishing their workout too, and they could all have breakfast together, reading various sections of the newspaper and chatting together about world events or what they had planned for the day, maybe relating a joke or two they'd heard, all smiling and buzzing, chit-chatting too fast from all the coffee they sipped.

Then it would be time for Dr. Ursa to shower and puff out his thick brown hair with a comb into a pleasing halo of clean fur, don his white coat, grab his small black leather doctor's bag, head out of the front door, nod to Pedro, then walk from one end of the building to the other, where his office and office manager Karen waited for him. If the wawas buzzed with early morning coffee, Karen practically whirred with it, so ready was she to start her day and make sure Dr. Ursa kept on track seeing all of his patients in a timely fashion.

***

Most days in the morning, after breakfast but before lunch, as well as in the evening, after teatime but before dinner, Mr. Rabbit and Benny would have quiet time in which to pursue their creative passions. Mr. Rabbit was a painter—well, a painter primarily; he sometimes delved into all variations of the visual arts. Over the years he had made papier-mâché versions of Benny and Dr. Ursa. He had constructed clay versions of some of the more interesting-looking groundhogs he had met when they had all lived in New Jersey, and, while accurate in physical proportions, he had taken liberties with the colors, glazing them a wild array of rainbow colors and firing them in a kiln, Raku style. He'd climbed a small tree in Central Park to take a beautifully composed photograph of a delicate nest amongst barely budding branches containing one striking blue robin's egg. He'd directed Dr. Ursa and Benny as actors in a short experimental film in which neither spoke but struck various dramatic poses edited together to create jarring juxtapositions and ending with them under the kitchen table lying on their sides facing each other, curled up holding their knees with blank expressions on their faces while a sunny-side-up fried egg dripped over the lip of the kitchen table down toward them, Salvador Dalí style. (While edited out of the film, the egg had actually fallen onto and stuck to Dr. Ursa's fur, and he'd let out a roar and retired from acting at that point to take a 45-minute bubble bath.)

But despite these diversions, Mr. Rabbit always came back to painting as his primary medium. Most quiet times you could find Mr. Rabbit having set up his easel in the living room of Apartment 1K, wearing an old chambray dress shirt unbuttoned and worn backward so that the back of the shirt faced forward to protect his fur from any flying paint, his eyes scrunched and focused as he furiously moved his straight arm about, painting the kaleidoscopic images in his brain. Some of his favorite subjects were the animals and nature he'd see as he walked in

24

Central Park or Riverside Park or on the occasions that he and Benny would take trips out to New Jersey. However, there was always some twist of imagery in the final product that went beyond portraiture.

On this particular day, Mr. Rabbit had decided to fully reconcile himself with the bee species after the incident in the dog park and paint the furry bumblebee that he had seen one day in the spring during one of his afternoon walks with Benny. The bumblebee had been having a grand old time jumping from flower to flower, pollinating the plants as he ate his lunchtime meal. But instead of painting the bee in the actual setting Mr. Rabbit had seen him, he made the painting's background shocks of color fading into the distance, emanating out in waves from the colors of the bee, the yellow and black of its stripes, the translucent white-gray of its wings. Then from the edges of the canvas, stabbing back as inward narrowing blotches, were the colors of the flowers—the pinks and purples and blues.

Mr. Rabbit loved to paint all sorts of things, but his favorite subject was Benny the Bunny. He had done an intensive study of some dozen portraits capturing Benny in all his many outward and internal angles—from action shots of Benny run-hopping through the great grasses of Central Park to still pieces where the wisdom of the world seemed to softly swirl about Benny's head in great clouds of enlightenment while the physical Benny sat quietly in a chair.

Not that Mr. Rabbit left Dr. Ursa or Pedro out. He had made a grandly large piece of Dr. Ursa sleeping on the couch with his white coat and stethoscope still on, so tired was he from the work day, his great bear belly rhythmically moving up and down, his enormous bear body seeming to radiate the safety he made Mr. Rabbit feel. And Mr. Rabbit had spent several obsessive days trying every trick in the book to somehow capture Pedro's smile with a close-up portrait piece. And though Pedro told Mr. Rabbit when he gave the painting to him that he felt it somehow captured him better than any picture, in the end Mr. Rabbit thought he maybe only got 98 percent of the way there, because there was just some element of warmth in Pedro's smile that could only be experienced in person.

While like all artists he sometimes got stuck, most days the paintings would fly out of Mr. Rabbit in one great heave of effort. As if he had hardly stopped for breath from start to finish. As if there was no thought, just a blazing image of shape and color that must be carved out of his mind and into existence on the canvas. For Mr. Rabbit, quiet time was anything but in his head; it was the searing flash of visual creation. And while he was at his painting, he felt brimming full of life and spirit. It was as if he was the conduit of some sacred eye to some subtle hand or paw. But once the creation was complete, the vast expenditure of mental energy would hit him all at once, and he'd hop down from his stool and curl up on the couch and fall fast asleep for a little nap until Benny woke him for lunch or dinner as the case may be.

While Mr. Rabbit painted, Benny worked on his mystery novel. Benny found it too distracting to try to write on his computer with all of the possibilities of the internet just a paw-click away. Sometimes he wrote longhand when necessary—if he was struck by inspiration while sitting on a park bench, for instance. But Benny found longhand too slow for regular writing. A typewriter was the best of both worlds. So during quiet time, Benny would furrow his brow and clack away at his blue-green Smith Corona typewriter.

Benny's relationship with the writing of his mystery novel was complex. The creative act was a necessary thing in his life. As necessary as eating or sleeping. While he wouldn't get hungry for writing as quickly as he'd get hungry if he skipped breakfast in the morning, and he wouldn't get sleepy from lack of writing as assuredly as if he stayed up too late watching movies, if he went too long without sitting behind his Smith Corona, some part of him would start to become sluggish, and then more sluggish, and eventually entirely stuck. The colors of the world would tint with gray. There would be unexplained headaches. He'd think, "I must be coming down with a cold." But then he'd remember: a stuffed rabbit must make time for creativity.

For Benny, creativity was writing. Sometimes he envied Mr. Rabbit for finding his artistic expression through painting. It seemed that Mr. Rabbit all but exploded with images and colors and ideas. While for Benny, writing was such a plodding thing. And often fraught with anxieties. Still, it was Benny's nature to write, just as it was Mr. Rabbit's nature to paint. When Benny sank into his writing, became lost in it, he felt fully himself. He needed at least a little dose of that feeling every day. So while there was often a temptation to skip quiet time, just like there might be to skip exercise time or stretching time, Benny did his best to keep as much quiet time on the schedule as possible.

26

There were peculiarities in the way Benny wrote. One particularly powerful peculiarity was that he couldn't have anyone behind him. There could be people in the room (and he often wrote in coffee shops while Mr. Rabbit furiously sketched on his sketch pad across from him, so focused he wouldn't notice the white foam from his latte covering his upper lip and sometimes even his pink nose) and he could read aloud the day's work to Mr. Rabbit or Dr. Ursa, but no one but himself could witness the words appearing on the typewriter paper. If he were in a coffee shop and couldn't find a seat with his back against the wall, his writing process would become completely paralyzed. And even if (as was most likely) the other patrons hadn't the slightest desire to read what he wrote, the mere fact that *they could* prevented him from getting anything done.

It was this sort of anxiousness that made writing such a contradictory exercise for Benny. It was both fraught with, but also a powerful relief from, anxiety. Almost like how jogging made you feel very tired and unmotivated when you contemplated beginning the jog but could make you feel proud and full of energy once you had finished.

The element of anxiety was particularly acute for Benny's current project. Being a mystery novel, Benny had created a villain character. Benny didn't very much like writing about villains, but in certain types of tales, they were unfortunately necessary. And while not entirely pleasant, they could be used to reveal certain truths. Benny's current villain was a diabolical history professor, but, since the book was a mystery novel, you didn't learn of his villainy until the very end. So there was the special challenge of burying his malice under a false layer of good-naturedness.

But while this particular villain was a human history professor, the root of each of Benny's villains all came from the same place, the same fear. They all came from The Wolf.

For as long as Benny could remember, there was The Wolf.

At first, The Wolf had no name. Was not really a wolf or even a clear image. The Wolf was just a pounding in Benny's ears while he tried to go to sleep. A pounding in time with his heartbeat as if counting out the time until … whatever it was to be would come for him. Some unspeakable demon from the dark under the bed or behind the closet door.

Then in dreams, sounds and images formed. A flash of a tooth. A rhythmic breath. A cold eye. A claw. A howl. Pulled-back lips and a mouth of teeth. Then that pounding sound in his ears at night formed a cohesive visual.

The Wolf.

Each heartbeat was The Wolf. Each heartbeat was a step or a breath as The Wolf hunted him. Benny reassured himself—The Wolf must be very far away; he was off on some different continent, some different planet, even. Half a galaxy away, maybe. But those reassurances were but a poor salve to his fear. He suspected that much as he might try to think him away, in the end, nothing would stop The Wolf coming for him. He'd cross space and oceans. He was inevitable. Each beat of Benny's heart brought The Wolf another step closer, another instant closer.

Inside every villain Benny created was The Wolf. And to sit down to write was to remember The Wolf. To remember that with every word Benny typed and with every word he didn't, The Wolf was coming.

And perhaps there was some magic in that. For without The Wolf, would Benny ever feel that great urgency, that unending need to create? Creation seemed to Benny like some great battle. Something brought back from the edge of things, where something-ness and nothingness collided, where the very brave might venture to bring about some new continent in the void.

***

The wawas were creatures of habit, but habits and rituals were always subject to the flux and whim of the universe. On this particular day, just as Mr. Rabbit was finishing his painting of the furry bumblebee, he heard Karen's elevated voice in the hallway. He thought, "Well, that's quite odd. Usually Karen and Dr. Ursa are working very hard to get to see all the different wawas that need a little help."

So Mr. Rabbit hopped toward Karen's voice, but before he even got through the French doors he heard a large bang as their front door swung open and Karen and Dr. Ursa loudly stomped into the vestibule. Karen quickly spotted Mr. Rabbit at the top of the stairs looking down at them.

"It's just like him!" she called up in obvious exasperation. "He's sick with a cold—if a patient had his symptoms, he would immediately put them on bed rest, but he's so busy whirling about he doesn't take the time to even recognize he's under the weather."

"Oh no," said Mr. Rabbit, mouth hanging open slightly in worried surprise.

"Yes! It's just like last winter." Karen looked from Mr. Rabbit back down to Dr. Ursa. "Don't you remember? Remember how you got a nasty flu and had to stay in bed for a week? You've got to start taking care of yourself without me having to make a harrumph."

By way of reply, Dr. Ursa let out an enormous bear sneeze.

With that, they were all flying into action, their normal routines completely forgotten. Dr. Ursa was soon positioned on the couch with a great soft blanket wrapped around him, a box of tissues on the armrest, a glass of water and orange juice on the coffee table. Mr. Rabbit was hunting around the bedroom for Dr. Ursa's wool-lined slippers, while Benny the Bunny heated up matzah ball soup and a kettle for green tea.

Karen paced around the living room, making call after call to cancel the afternoon's patients and make referrals when necessary to the other wawatrician on the Upper West Side, a golden retriever wawa named Dr. Puddles.

Once all was arranged for Dr. Ursa's comfort, Mr. Rabbit and Benny sat around the kitchen table to listen to Karen vent about the day's frustrations.

Mr. Rabbit and Benny both loved Karen very much. Her face was crafted with soft, pleasing curves, punctuated with fiercely focused eyes, and framed with long straight blonde hair that crowned her meticulously put-together outfits. She was tough and sometimes frazzled on the outside, but for her that was necessary to make sure things got done and that her large, loving heart would have some protection from the elements. No one cared more for Dr. Ursa and all of his wawa patients than Karen, and being filled with all that caring could be a great burden.

Both Mr. Rabbit and Benny the Bunny knew all about that.

***

Once things settled down, Dr. Ursa had finished eating and drinking and was soundly snoring in the bedroom, Karen said farewell to the rabbits and they were left to try to figure out how to go about their day, with their usual routine completely abandoned.

"What would you like to do?" Benny asked Mr. Rabbit. "I suppose we shouldn't go far to make sure we're here in case Dr. Ursa needs some help."

"Hmmm, I guess if you wouldn't mind, I'd like to do another portrait of you. Would you mind terribly to sit and pose for me?"

"Of course not," replied Benny the Bunny.

And so Benny sat in a comfy chair in the living room looking out of the window at the late autumn sky, at the brown leaves jostling in the wind, the last stubborn leaves that still managed to hang on.

As he sat and watched the outside, hearing the swooping and scratching sounds of Mr. Rabbit's painting, Benny reflected on a trying incident the week before. Mr. Rabbit had gotten the idea that perhaps others might enjoy seeing some of his paintings, so Benny and Mr. Rabbit had hustled onto the downtown train to SoHo. Mr. Rabbit had researched a gallery there full of paintings he quite liked where he thought he might ask if one of his paintings might be displayed. Benny was cautious as they rode downtown, knowing how difficult these things could be, but Mr. Rabbit was brimming with excitement, smiling widely at all of the faces he saw in the subway.

Mr. Rabbit had brought with him *Benny the Bunny No. 16*, the already-mentioned portrait of Benny thinking in a chair, being one of Mr. Rabbit's particular favorites. Mr. Rabbit carried the painting as they walked along in SoHo, where both rabbits found themselves taken in by all the wondrous fashion displayed in the storefronts and swishing by them on the streets.

But inside the gallery they found only disappointment. At first the clerk had refused to go into the back to ask the gallery curator to look at the painting, but with much heartfelt pleading, she finally relented. Benny suspected that behind her standoffish exterior, the clerk had been trying to protect Mr. Rabbit from the curator, for when he hustled out with an air of total annoyance, he barely glanced at Mr. Rabbit's painting, declared, "No one wants second-rate stuffed animal portraits," and disappeared as quickly as he came. The clerk at least had the decency to shrug her shoulders as if to say "I told you so" and "what a jerk" in the same silent movement.

The thing that pulled at Benny's heartstrings the most was the way it took so long for sadness to register on Mr. Rabbit's face. He stood there, still holding the painting up even after the curator had disappeared once more, the smile Mr. Rabbit had greeted the curator with now frozen on his face. Then, finally, Benny had put an arm around him, and his soft furry face had fallen and a vacant look had come into his eyes.

That same look was still there on Mr. Rabbit's downcast face as they sat together on the subway heading back uptown. Benny felt powerless to do or say anything to make him feel better. But as he looked out at the varied faces he saw all about the subway car, a thought came to him, and he leaned over to whisper in Mr. Rabbit's floppy ear.

"Look at all the different people on the subway. Aren't they something? All different in appearance. Isn't the temptation to look at them all and see them only in the now, as *being* as they *appear*? Expressionless. Looking at their phones. Impatient. But that's not who they *are*. Not really. That's just a moment. I like to look at them and imagine all the things they've felt. That grumpy young man over there, there was a time he cried all night when the girl he loved explained she didn't love him back. The older woman over there, she's gone through losing both of her parents, feels the pain of it still, but carries on nonetheless. That young mother who is so harried by her children, she's ridden a roller coaster and screamed in joy. They've all been disappointed. They've all felt joy. They're all sometimes nostalgic, sometimes careless. They all dread and hope for the future. They've all been bone tired. But they've all been bursting with energy and excitement too. Sure, you might find a rare person that's the exception. But almost universally, we all share in these things. And whatever might possess us in the moment, however we might try not to look at each other in this subway car … I think we all somehow share the same heart."

Mr. Rabbit hadn't said anything in return; he had just laid his head down to rest on Benny's shoulder and Benny had put his arm around him again.

Then the next day Mr. Rabbit had gone right back to painting.

And he had not missed a single day since. And Benny knew as he watched Mr. Rabbit's resilience and courage to create, that some day Mr. Rabbit's paintings would get the recognition they deserved. Perhaps one fine day they would even be displayed in some grand exhibit. He thought, "I should take Mr. Rabbit for a special outing soon, maybe to The Rabbit Diner. He deserves to have a nice little treat."

As Benny sat there, listening to the sounds of Mr. Rabbit painting and looking out at the gray skies and the brown leaves and the fading fall all around, he found himself tearing up a little thinking about all that Mr. Rabbit brought to his life and of all his quiet courage.

Seeing Benny's tears, Mr. Rabbit knew them for tears of happiness and drew them as precious diamonds sparkling in a great river that flowed from Benny's eyes, filling the world with one more beautiful thing.

The Rabbit Diner

Big wet snowflakes that just about bowled Mr. Rabbit over relentlessly pounded Riverside Park. He clutched at Benny the Bunny's paw as he tottered along as best he could. It was tough to really hop in all this snow and while wearing thick boots.

They had known snow was coming. But not so soon or so much.

They were prepared with boots and big coats and warm knit hats. And while Mr. Rabbit couldn't see much besides the general mess of flakes that periodically hit his eyes and turned the world to water (and also periodically hit his tongue with much more refreshing results), he could make out the warm yellow glow of The Rabbit Diner. And for this, his heart was glad.

When they finally made it all the way to that warm glow and opened the front door into the entranceway, it was as if they brought a squall of snow with them. But quickly the two wawas pressed their weight back against the door and were able to seal themselves off from the outside. Slowly, Mr. Rabbit acclimatized to his new surroundings. There was that warm yellow light all around him now, and he felt as if the warm light was entering through his fur and heating him back up from within. As his eyes began to adjust to the change in light between outside and inside, The Rabbit Diner came into focus.

The Rabbit Diner was one of those utterly unique New York dining institutions. The humans had Delmonico's, Katz's Deli, La Grenouille, Barney Greengrass, and the 21 Club. The rabbits had The Rabbit Diner. And for the rabbits, it was somehow like all of those human institutions wrapped into one.

Both wild and the far less common wawa rabbits were welcome, but every gentlerabbit had to wear a jacket. So when Benny the Bunny and Mr. Rabbit had finished stripping off their outwear and storing it, boots and all, with the matronly coat check attendant, whose whiskers had twitched with disapproval at our two heroes as they had knocked the snow off their fur and all over the entranceway floor, they were revealed to be wearing a somewhat more formal accouterment than was their norm. Mr. Rabbit sported a sumptuous blue blazer with mother-of-pearl buttons and no tie, while Benny the Bunny hinted at his more bucolic upbringing with a gray herringbone sport coat and dark green knit tie worn without a shirt, as was the rabbit fashion.

From the entranceway, Benny and Mr. Rabbit let themselves into the dining room proper. Standing at his post, they were greeted by a gruff but kindly and somewhat overweight gray French Lop rabbit named George. As was the case with all servers and hosts in The Rabbit Diner, George wore a formal black waistcoat, a black coat with tails, and a white bow tie. (The bartenders were the exception, being classically appointed in charcoal vests, white shirts, and black sleeve garters.)

George couldn't help but smile a bit when he saw Benny the Bunny and Mr. Rabbit, who happened to be two of his favorite customers, both for their regularity and their calm demeanors. Some patrons of The Rabbit Diner could get a bit out of hand, especially some of the younger hares during the later hours of operation. George had little patience for those types.

"Counter, bar, tavern, or dining?" asked George, by which he meant to ask which portion of the diner would they be occupying this evening: the counter was a traditional diner counter; the bar a place to socialize and take a mixed drink, like the ever-popular beet juice and soda with a lemon twist; the tavern was for casual dining; and the dining room, with its tables draped in white cloth and candles burning, was for more formal affairs.

"Tavern, please," said Benny the Bunny. "A booth would be perfect—something tucked away if you can."

"I think I have just the thing," George replied.

George grabbed two menus and the two wawas followed him into the tavern as he waddled at a surprisingly quick pace, his big fluffy white ball of a tail poking out between the two tails of his coat and his heavy lop ears bouncing up and down with each step.

Mr. Rabbit was very excited to see a celebrity in the local rabbit community, Jacque Janssen, lounging in a half-circle booth with several much smaller rabbit friends. Jacque Janssen was a Flemish Giant, a truly enormous breed of rabbit a little bigger even than a medium-sized dog. Jacque was telling a story that was, if the reaction of his friends was to be believed, uproariously funny, while he lay against the booth back, both arms thrown up over the edges of the booth. Mr. Rabbit made a subtle head gesture to Benny the Bunny to look over there.

Catching on, Benny looked, and his eyes went a bit wide and a sly little smile came to his lips. He bent to whisper in Mr. Rabbit's ear, "He's certainly a Flemish *Giant*. Odd how such a small country has such enormous rabbits."

The booth George finally brought them to was indeed perfect. Tucked in a corner where they could feel warm and cozy, a part of the crowd but also a bit removed. Perfect for a little relaxation and a nice chat.

When their waiter came over, they ordered a big bowl of what the menu called *fraise mit schlag*—a strange combination of French and German words meaning strawberries with whipped cream. Only the whipped cream was freshly hand-whipped and done in that thick luxurious manner of southern Germany, while the strawberries were so delicate and bursting with tart flavor, they required their French name to truly convey the specialness of the experience.

"I'm so excited," Mr. Rabbit said. "*Fraise mit schlag* is my favorite! I love the way they serve it here with the tops still on the strawberries like rabbits like it. Humans always cut that part off."

"A cardinal sin in rabbit culinary circles," replied Benny.

"That's right!" said Mr. Rabbit, moving excitedly about in his seat a bit, filled with anticipation for his favorite dish. Fortunately, The Rabbit Diner prided itself on fast and efficient service, so their waiter soon returned with a big bowl of *fraise mit schlag* and two steaming mugs of tea to wash it down with.

Mr. Rabbit's anticipation for *fraise mit schlag* had built up in the back of his mind over the last week after Benny had promised to take him to The Rabbit Diner just as soon as Dr. Ursa had fully recovered from his recent cold. And while Mr. Rabbit had been quite dutifully focused on his friend's recovery, once Dr. Ursa had felt completely better and bored with lying in bed or on the couch all day, reading or watching movies, and had begun to complain that he was already better enough to get back to work yesterday, Mr. Rabbit had let the idea of *fraise mit schlag* move from the back of his mind to the front. Once there, it began to dominate his thinking. In fact, on the day of The Rabbit Diner outing, Mr. Rabbit had spent the whole morning and afternoon with luscious strawberries and luxurious cream floating and undulating about in his mind's eye.

By the time his *fraise mit schlag* was set before him, all that building anticipation had reached a boiling point within Mr. Rabbit so that he found himself having a very difficult time controlling the speed at which he shoveled down his strawberries and whipped cream, taking only quick heavy breathing breaks and periodically sipping his tea.

Benny sat back, blew the steam off his tea, and let his friend enjoy himself. Moderation was best most days, but a little excess was just the thing every once in a while. Once Mr. Rabbit had slowed down enough that Benny thought he might be able safely extricate a strawberry without bumping into Mr. Rabbit's ravenous paw, he grabbed one with a healthy portion of whipped cream, brought it to his mouth, and chewed it slowly, thoughtfully, enjoying each burst of flavor and texture.

Finishing his bite, he said, "You know, Mr. Rabbit, watching you eat is reminding me of my old friend Custerd, the orange wawa cat I told you about."

Mr. Rabbit paused and almost seemed to blush underneath his fur. "Oh—oh yes. I remember some of the stories you've told me about him."

"Did I tell you the one about the Easter eggs?"

"I don't think so," said Mr. Rabbit between large mouthfuls of delicious *fraise mit schlag*.

So Benny told Mr. Rabbit a story from the old days when he, Custerd, and Rogo the lion had all lived together in Massachusetts. About painting Easter eggs and how Benny had struggled to do a very good job with the painting, the visual arts not being one of his talents. Still, between the whole gang, they had painted some really beautiful ones—all sorts of wonderful pastel colors, light greens and blues and pinks. Some were a solid color, some half one color, half another, some striped, some polka-dotted. And Benny had loved the Easter egg hunt the next day too. But before it was over, Custerd and the others had gotten quite distracted by all of the Easter chocolates and candies, so that in the end, Benny had found himself out alone searching for the last beautiful painted eggs in the spring grass as dusk fell all around. Benny could still remember all of those uniquely colored eggs dazzling all the colors of the rainbow from his swinging wicker basket, like precious jewels he'd snatched from the encroaching darkness.

And he could still remember how lonely he had felt too.

Mr. Rabbit, feeling bad for his friend's lack of egg-painting talent, told a story about how a group of friendly groundhogs once tried to teach him how to dig really excellent holes in the ground, but unfortunately, Mr. Rabbit's delicate front paws were not particularly suited for large digging operations, and he had wound up spending the majority of his time lying on the grass, sipping iced tea, and having a nice chat with whichever groundhogs happened to be taking a break.

"Aren't rabbits supposed to be good diggers?" Mr. Rabbit asked.

"Well, I suppose some rabbits are quite good diggers," replied Benny.

Mr. Rabbit sat silently for a while, thinking about the implications of his lack of digging talent.

"Am I not quite really as I should be, then? I mean to say … shouldn't I be a good digger if I'm a good rabbit?"

"You're an excellent rabbit!" said Benny. "Just like Jacque Janssen is a good rabbit in his way, being uniquely large and charming and, I imagine, an exemplary digger. You are an excellent rabbit in your own way. Full of courage and friendship and wonderfully creative images to paint. I couldn't imagine a more excellent rabbit, in fact."

A smile came to Mr. Rabbit's face, and to Benny that smile seemed to glow with a beautiful light that was made only more special by all the whipped cream that was stuck to the fur around Mr. Rabbit's mouth.

"I think you're an excellent rabbit too," said Mr. Rabbit, who felt much the same about the smile on Benny's face as Benny did about his.

***

By the time Benny and Mr. Rabbit departed The Rabbit Diner, once again all bundled up in their outerwear, the snow had stopped actively falling. Still it was quite an effort for the rabbits to make their way through some of the larger snowdrifts that had accumulated. So difficult, in fact, that at one point Mr. Rabbit lost his footing and fell nose first into a big pile of snow. He squirmed his body around in order to get the necessary leverage to flip himself onto his back. By the time he managed to get himself all the way turned around, with a little help from Benny, and had oriented himself, he realized Benny was lying down beside him in the snow.

"Hey, Benny," Mr. Rabbit said, looking over at his friend and smiling.

"Hey, Mr. Rabbit," Benny said, returning the smile. "Want to make snow angels?"

"I thought you'd never ask," replied Mr. Rabbit.

The rabbits moved their arms and legs up and down, all the while looking up at twisting black tree branches covered in stark white snow. The world was cold. But with their winter clothes and the insulating snow and their bellies full—it was warm inside the rabbits.

An Unexpected Visitor

It was bright and warm inside, but outside it drizzled in the cold dark. Mr. Rabbit was on a Persian rug halfway through his evening stretches, while Benny stitched up the torn red strap of his green overalls. Benny concentrated very deeply on his sewing. Sewing is an important skill for a stuffed rabbit. Benny thought that when something was important, one should give their whole focus over to it, even when they had done it many times before.

While Benny concentrated very fixedly on his sewing, Mr. Rabbit's mind was differently disposed as he went through his stretching routine. It was as if his thoughts were lost in the movement of his body. As if he needn't think at all. Of course there were some thoughts in his head, but they were just passing fancies. Feelings that floated through his mind light as soap bubbles. "Mmmmmmm," he thought as he stretched his big fluffy feet. "Hmmmmmm." It felt very nice to stretch his feet. They did so much for him all day long and it was so wonderful to be able to do something nice for them. And "Ahhhhhhh," he thought when he heard the light drizzle outside, and the darkness out there was thrown back by the lamplight every time it tried to sneak in the window. And how it must be cold outside, but he was so safe and warm here inside. Just over his shoulder there was Benny making pleasant little scratching noises as he oh so carefully made each stitch. And back in the bedroom, Dr. Ursa was already asleep with his book lying open against his chest.

"Mmmmmm," thought Mr. Rabbit some more. And then, "Mmmmmm, this is so very nice." And then a very different thought came into his head. "What's that?" he thought.

Mr. Rabbit thought "What's that?" because there was a loud thumping noise coming from the vestibule downstairs. Mr. Rabbit paused his stretch just as he was bent over reaching unsuccessfully for his toes with his white tail twitching in the air.

Thump, thump, came the noise from the vestibule.

Mr. Rabbit raised himself back up from his stretch and looked over at Benny. The older rabbit hadn't seemed to hear the noise, so concentrated was he on his stitching. "Better not disturb him," thought Mr. Rabbit as he hopped along through the French doors and down the stairs to his front door.

"I bet it's Pedro," he thought. Sometimes Pedro would knock when they got a special package in. "Hmm, I wonder what we got in the mail. Maybe Benny bought some treats for us. Maybe it's some special surprise. Wouldn't that be very nice?"

When Mr. Rabbit got to the bottom of the stairs, he hopped up on the bannister so that he could reach the doorknob. When he turned the knob and poked his head around the corner, he was rather surprised to see a great moon of orange fluff staring back at him. Mr. Rabbit was startled for a moment but quickly found his composure, blinked his eyes and refocused them. What he saw was this: a somewhat stout stuffed cat with worn orange fur, a bulbous black nose, big white eyes with pinpoint pupils, and a wide smile with a lolling pink tongue. The ears were tiny uneven triangles plopped on the sides of a great round head. The head sat upon a great round ball of a torso that Mr. Rabbit thought was very pleasing to the eye. The cat had short arms and legs and was sitting on the top rung of a stepladder that Pedro was bent down holding so it wouldn't tip over. There was a large white box in the cat's arms with a red bow on it. But the bow seemed to be somewhat disheveled and tied together in a slapdash manner.

It took Mr. Rabbit so long to take in all that was before him that he only just caught on that the cat was speaking to him. Or to Pedro. Or to anyone who happened to be there. His voice was low but sharp, as if it flew through a windpipe that could barely contain it. It sounded joyous and delightful to Mr. Rabbit. Words came rapid fire, but before long his ears began to track the words down and make sense of them.

"... and yes, Pedro here was good enough to help with the boost. Yes, yes, yes, thank you so much, Pedro. I'll be sure to get you that number for Wally's Confectionary for your grandmother's birthday. Such a wonderful thing, chocolates, especially when done right. And grandmothers too, for the most part. Yes, yes, yes, as I was saying, so here I am. In the fur, so to speak. And where did you say my good pal Benny was? I was expecting him at the door. Could you please help an old cat out? Oh yes, your name. I seemed to have forgotten to ask ... I brought chocolates ... or I brought a *box* of chocolates. The chocolates themselves seem to have gone missing. Well ..."

The cat shook the box. Mr. Rabbit made out a few lonely rattles within.

"… there may be a couple left that are possibly filled with a kind of lemon flavoring. And something seems to have left some tooth marks in those, but I'm sure Benny will enjoy them nonetheless. Yes, yes, yes, when are you going to invite me in? I've been in the rain, you know."

Finally, more than a breath of time was left open for Mr. Rabbit to get a word in.

"Um, hello," he said.

"Hello," said the cat quizzically.

"I'm Mr. Rabbit. It's um, nice to meet you. What's your name?"

"What?" yelled the orange cat. "Benny must have regaled you with my exploits. The old devil."

Mr. Rabbit gave the cat another look over and it slowly came to him that the cat was right. He knew exactly who this orange cat was. How could he have been so silly not to see it immediately?

"Custerd?" he asked.

"That's right, you big fur ball! The one, the only! Now, who's going to help me with my bags?"

So it was that Mr. Rabbit found himself hopping back up the stairs struggling to carry a Mr. Rabbit–sized leopard printed purse, while Pedro hauled up two enormous suit bags and Custerd restricted himself to the almost-empty box of chocolates. Custerd charged ahead of Pedro and Mr. Rabbit, so Mr. Rabbit could see his long straight tail wagging with his movements. It looked as though someone had rubbed the tail very many times and the end of it had frayed. Mr. Rabbit thought that the fraying tail did not detract from Custerd's appearance but instead lent him a distinguished air.

Reaching the top of the stairs moments before Mr. Rabbit hopped there himself, Custerd declared, "Benny! Oh, Benny! Where's my long-limbed rapscallion rabbit friend?"

Mr. Rabbit caught sight of a startled look on Benny's face as he looked up from his stitching. When Benny saw Custerd so suddenly appearing in his living room, his already straight ears seemed to straighten even more and extend an extra centimeter or two from his head, and his soulful black eyes went wide, and even his mouth momentarily hung open as if his jaw had fallen involuntarily slack.

"Hi ho, there's the bunny I'm looking for!" called Custerd.

For a second or two, Benny seemed unable to get his mouth to form words, but finally said softly in a tone one octave higher than his normal voice, "Custerd. You're here. You're here and … you've brought chocolates."

"A *box* of chocolates, Señor Benny. I was just explaining to our mutual acquaintance *Mr.* Rabbit that the chocolates themselves have seemed to run off."

Benny hopped down from his chair at the kitchen table and started to move toward Custerd. It seemed to Mr. Rabbit that Benny moved almost in slow motion. And his head appeared to be floating a bit, like he was in a deep think and not really looking at the world around him. Meanwhile when Custerd, after a brief repartee with Pedro thanking him for all of his services and making jokes about the weight of his equipage, turned his attention back to the approaching rabbit, he let out a loud chortle, tossed the box of chocolates to the side, and bounded into Benny's hastily opening arms, knocking Benny to a seated position on the ground with his momentum.

Mr. Rabbit felt a thrill of emotion as he took a mental snapshot of the image in front of him. Benny was pinioned against the side of the couch, with hindquarters propped on the ground and his legs stretched out. Custerd was like a large orange ball curled up on Benny's lap. Custerd's short arms strained to reach out and grasp Benny, while Benny's enveloped him in a hug. Custerd buried his head in Benny's chest and rubbed it slightly up and down. There was a noticeable "prrrrrrrrrrr" emanating not just from Custerd's mouth but from the totality of Custerd's body. Mr. Rabbit couldn't quite see Custerd's face, but on Benny's face there was a half-quizzical, half-relaxed smile and the glistening of wetness about his beautiful black eyes.

Mr. Rabbit thought about the emotion he saw and the emotion he felt. Benny's tears were of joy, he thought. It was a very happy reunion. But there was also something rather sad about the moment too. A sadness in Benny's expression and the way Mr. Rabbit's own emotions mixed joy and sorrow. He couldn't put his finger on it. A wild thought ran through his mind. He thought, "It's like they are enjoying this hug as much as one could enjoy a hug, but also as if they know they are only allotted 10,000 such hugs with one another and they're on 1,374 and they can't bear to think that there is now one less to go." Mr. Rabbit shivered a bit and then shook the shiver out of his body. That wasn't the right way to think about it, was it? Who could know how many hugs there were going to be? And couldn't you hug all that you might want? But he wasn't exactly sure how to think about it properly, and it wasn't the right time to ask Benny to explain it all in that slow, wise way of his. The only thing he could really conclude without any doubt, with a bit of water coming to his eyes as well, was that it was a beautiful hug.

Benny and Custerd eventually straightened themselves out. Dusting himself off, Custerd proclaimed, "Well, aren't you going to offer an old cat some tea and sssssscrumpets? There's lots to talk about, and warm liquids would do just the trick in easing it all along."

"What a delightful idea!" thought Mr. Rabbit. So Mr. Rabbit and Custerd seated themselves at the kitchen table while Benny cleared off his sewing, then retreated to the kitchen proper to prepare the tea and whatever sssssscrumpets were.

"What are sssssscrumpets?" asked Mr. Rabbit.

"Hohoho," said Custerd. "Sssssscrumpets are my little word for 'scrumptious crumpets.' To be completely frank, I'm not 100 percent sure what crumpets really are, but I think they're anything that's sweet and baked and somewhat crumbly in your mouth and go just wonderfully with tea."

"Oooooo, that does sound wonderful," said Mr. Rabbit.

"Would old Custerd lead you astray? Hohoho, perish the thought, my dear cottontail."

"What sort of tea would *y'all* like?" Benny called from the kitchen, affecting a slight southern twang. This popped up every now and again with Benny, mostly to cover his general discomfort with the lack of a proper second person plural in the English language. "We have Earl Grey, English Breakfast, Constant Comment ..."

"Woooo, I'll have the Constant *Comet*, please," yelled Custerd.

46

"The same for me," said Mr. Rabbit, thinking it would be very nice to learn a thing or two from Custerd about the enjoyment of libations and culinary delights.

There was a din of pots clanging in the kitchen while Benny went about his task. Meanwhile, Custerd and Mr. Rabbit regarded each other for a long moment. There was a feeling on Mr. Rabbit's part that Custerd was for the first time really attempting to plumb Mr. Rabbit's character. A mutual respect was already blossoming, he thought. And it was so nice to have an old friend of Benny's as a visitor. What lovely things they would have to talk about!

"Tea!" cried Benny, carrying a round silver tray into the room, then sliding it onto the table. There were three teacups and saucers of various provenances, mismatched, as was their traditional style at Apartment 1K. There was their lovely Canton teapot. There was a little white cup of milk and a small jar of very dark, very sweet honey that Benny and Mr. Rabbit had bought at a country general store while hiking in the Delaware Water Gap. ("Mmmmm," Mr. Rabbit thought as he remembered the strawberry rhubarb pie they had bought at that general store as well.) There were also about nine of the chocolate chip cookies Benny and Mr. Rabbit had baked the night before.

Mr. Rabbit's heart beat a bit faster at the thought of having more of the cookies. He had almost forgotten about them! Looking over at him, Custerd's eyes had grown wide as well, and there was noticeable saliva gathering at the edges of his mouth.

"Perhaps not the traditional teatime pastry, but it's not quite teatime and it's all we had," Benny explained.

A whole cookie was already stuffed in Custerd's mouth, the crumbs flying everywhere. "What was that? I seem to have become distracted by this chocolate sssscrumpet."

"Nothing of import," Benny replied.

Benny poured the tea—first for Custerd, then for Mr. Rabbit, who tapped the table by his cup with his paw to say "thank you" in the Chinese style, then finally for himself. He replaced the pot on the table, then situated himself in his chair. Custerd paused momentarily from inhaling cookies to drop a smidge of milk in his tea, followed by a long, snorting squeeze of the dark country honey.

For a moment there was only the sound of their small spoons scraping the insides of their teacups in light little circles as they mixed in their chosen proportions of milk and honey. Then Benny broke the silence. "Custerd, I can't tell you what a wonderful surprise it is to have you visit. It's been far, far too long. How's Boca Raton? I would have thought this would be the perfect time of year to be out of the New York weather and in the Florida sun. What brings you up this way?"

"I thought you'd never ask!" burst Custerd. "And has everything to do with *you*, my old rabbit friend. Well, you and Rogo, to be precise."

"Rogo!" Now it was Benny's turn to almost burst. "Have ... have you seen him?"

"Seen Rogo! Of course not, and that's precisely the point."

"But if you haven't seen him, then ..."

"Precisely the point! Benny, my dear old rabbit, we must find him! Bring him home. It's time."

Benny sat back in his chair. Was quiet a moment.

"Well, let me tell you the whole story. It's like I can't get a word in edgewise!" cried Custerd. And so it was that Benny and Mr. Rabbit sat back in their chairs, sipping tea and nibbling on cookies with their little pursed mouths while the rain pitter-pattered in the cold outside, and listened to Custerd. Custerd, meanwhile, told the story of the recent revelations that led to his unannounced visit to New York City, while swigging tea and taking brief breaks to gobble down cookies and even briefer breathing breaks.

***

Custerd was walking the beach in Boca. He had his third-favorite Hawaiian shirt buttoned sporadically on, a straw hat with little holes carved out for his ears, and he felt empty.

Custerd was used to an emptiness of stomach. In fact, delighted in it. For when his stomach was empty, there was the chance to fill it again. But as he walked along, feeling the warm powdery sand on his paws, it wasn't his stomach that felt empty. In fact, he'd just gorged himself on chilidogs and Diet Coke from a nearby food stand and was, if anything, the opposite of empty of stomach. Perhaps verging on a bit sick.

If he wasn't empty of stomach, what was he empty of? He wasn't empty of head, that was for sure. In fact, part of the emptiness seemed to come from all those things that filled his head. There were about a thousand half-formed thoughts hurtling about in there to the point of just about making him dizzy. He thought the thoughts would settle down and learn to wait their turn if he indulged in a nice relax on the beach, but it wasn't having much of an effect so far.

Custerd plopped himself down on the sand and looked out at the water. The waves came in and out. There was something relaxing in that. The water coming up and receding was like a steady breath. Hypnotizing. He absentmindedly rubbed his right front paw in the sand. There was a white, almost translucent crab whose home was in the path of the breath-like water. Every time the water would recede, the crab would pop up out of his hole, then, when the water would steam back toward him, he would rush back under the sand to safety. Custerd became even more hypnotized watching the endless, repetitive motion of the crab.

"I'm not empty of stomach. And I'm not empty of head. Then what am I empty of?" thought Custerd. The world disappeared for a moment, maybe more, as those words bumbled about in his head. However long it was, he snapped to attention at the sound of a sharp clacking noise. The crab! The crab was attacking him!

Indeed, the crab had snuck up on Custerd in his distraction and was menacing him with his large pincer claw. Custerd scrambled to his feet. Juked left and right, all the while squeaking, "I say!" and "Good fellow, please!" and "Ahhhh!"

Custerd's rotund body was surprisingly lithe, and the crab's claw only managed to snap against the air as he moved to and fro, then ran from the shore, clutching at his straw hat, which threatened to fly away in the wind. A few paces inland and the crab gave up its assault and returned back to his hole and to his life of endless repetition. The waves coming in and out. The crab going up and down, in and out of his hole. His motivation as unknowable a mystery as black hole singularities or anything else you might imagine.

Custerd, huffing and puffing, decided he'd had enough of the beach for the day. Went home to his condominium complex. As he was about to open the door into his comfortable two-bedroom (he used the second bedroom as a den, which meant in practice that he slept in there almost as much as in the main bedroom, but on the couch curled up in a warm sunspot that appeared there in the afternoon hours), he saw Janice, his next-door neighbor, just leaving her condo.

"Hi there, Custerd. How's it going today?" Janice asked.

"Janice," Custerd replied. "Janice, I don't even know where to begin. The chilidogs, the crab—not the kind you eat—well, I'm not really sure he's not the kind you eat, but nonetheless, he wasn't in eating condition—and all the while this kind of emptiness. And not emptiness of stomach or head, I've determined. Oh, I mean, Janice, I'm at the beach, is what I'm trying to say, minding my own business, full of food and thoughts but empty of something, and this crazed crab attacks me for no earthly reason. It's possible that I may have been aimlessly tossing sand at it, but it's sort of the crab's fault in the end, when you think how it went about hypnotizing me with its in and out and in and out of its hole. I mean, come on, build your hole just a little further from the water and you're golden, you know what I'm saying, Janice. Anyways, it was a perfectly lovely day at the beach before this crab turned crabby, hohoho. But hey, that's crabs for you, I guess."

"Custerd, you think he was trying to pinch that ample orange behind of yours?" Janice said with a wry smile. Janice was a real card.

"Hohoho," laughed Custerd. "That's exactly what he was up to."

"But what was this about you feeling empty when you were feeling full?" asked Janice, her expression turning serious.

So Custerd tried to explain. Tried to say how it was nice when his stomach was empty and he got to eat again, and nice when his mind emptied out of thoughts and took a break. But it wasn't so nice to feel this emptiness he couldn't quite put his paw on. This emptiness that seemed to come from everywhere and nowhere at the same time.

"Custerd," Janice said when he had finished. "I think you're ready to join the club."

"What do you mean?" cried Custerd. "There's a club? I'm not a member already? What's the story here? Doesn't everyone remember the Oktoberfest party I threw this fall? Smashing success. I wore the lederhosen and there were fresh buttered pretzels and ..."

"… I'm giving you my therapist's number. He's the best. A bit stiff, but the best. He's who you see when you feel like that. That's the club I mean. About half the complex goes to see a therapist. Then we all gossip about it after. It's great fun."

And thus within a week of running into Janice, Custerd found himself sitting on Dr. Cilento's well-worn cloth couch in his second-favorite Hawaiian shirt.

Dr. Cilento had spent years working as a therapist in the Navy. He unmistakably had the bearing of a military man. Close-cropped hair. Thick, functional glasses. He sat very straight, without the slightest hint of movement of body or face. While this all might have been intimidating, somehow in Dr. Cilento's case it had the opposite effect. There was something comforting in his overall bearing. You knew he was watching closely. Would not jump to any false conclusions. He would judge. There was no doubt about that. Even if that wasn't in fashion these days. But he would be fair. And to whatever extent fairness allowed, he would be merciful.

"I'd like to hear that part again," Dr. Cilento was saying. "The part about Rogo."

"Well, as I said, he was a good friend," Custerd replied. "You see, there were many years before Benny came into the picture, and it was just me and Rogo. Rogo was a stuffed lion, but smaller than me. Still, he had great confidence. A lion's pride, if you will. And an even greater sense of humor. Benny and I can certainly enjoy a laugh, but Rogo's sense of humor was a little more cutting, a little more devious. Scratched a different itch, so to speak. Then he was taken away to college. Very hard on me. Benny was around at that point, so I still had a companion. Still, I knew it was just part of growing up and that eventually we'd all be together again.

"So, Rogo's at college and is taken away to Australia for a semester abroad. We couldn't have been more excited for him. What an adventure! Halfway around the globe. Benny had come quite a distance when he first arrived, but I was American born. It was hard to imagine the scope of a journey like that when I hadn't left our sleepy New England town in fifteen years. Anyhoo, we're all excited. A little nervous, but mostly excited. We're dying to hear the stories. To hear about the koalas and the kangaroos and the wombats and then about the koalas again.

"Then Rogo's boy returns from his semester in Australia. Benny and I are waiting at the front door just about steaming with excitement. I mean, I can hardly breathe. And I can't help but feel a large amount of guilt because I remember thinking, 'I wonder what wonderful little gifts he'll have brought me from the land down under' and things like that. Not really focused on Rogo himself the way a good cat should have been.

"Anyways, you know the rest. The boy arrives. There's no Rogo. The boy seems sad, but not devastated. 'Oh, Rogo was lounging in bed one day. The maid came and swept up all the sheets and took Rogo with her. I ran down into the laundry room. I searched everywhere, but he was gone.' Like what? I mean, Doc, to this day I can't use a maid service."

"And you've never heard from him or of him since?"

"That's right."

"And when you were taken to college. What was that like?"

"Oh, it was mostly fine. Sometimes college was a bit rough. Too many people in and out of the dorm room. A cat couldn't help but get jostled and tossed about a bit. Plus college was in upstate New York. I just about froze my tail off. Part of the reason I love Boca. After all of those years in the northeast ... I'm a warm-weather cat through and through."

"How's your relationship with Benny these days?"

"Well, we talk on the phone. Not daily. But when we get the chance. And we visit with one another. A holiday here and there. But he's up in New York City. He's got a whole life up there and I've got a whole life down here."

"Why do you think you don't live closer to one another?"

"You know how it is. You get older, you grow in your own way, you want your own things. Believe me, a cat like me could have a good time in New York, but when all's said and done, I'm a Boca cat. And sometimes I think ... I don't know. Like it would be too intense if we were all around each other again. Like I'm too much. Or that we both wouldn't be ... free. We would trap each other or something. Am I making sense?"

"In our conversation you returned to Benny and Rogo again and again. This says to me that you are missing something from your past. Literally manifested in the missing Rogo but also in the distance between Benny and yourself. And the two of you already know each other's location. Do you know what you seem to be saying to me?"

"Yes," Custerd replied brightly, but then paused. "I mean no."

"You came in here and said you were empty. Psychologically empty. Profoundly empty. It seems to me that the past still haunts you. That you've settled into a routine. That you have good friends and good fun. But that you're also preparing yourself. Preparing yourself for the great adventure that awaits. The one that will tie you and Benny back together. And if I were to guess, he's up in New York waiting for the same thing—for the moment when you both have finally readied yourself to go out into the world together. To search for what you lost so long ago. To search for Rogo. Who can say whether you'll find him again or not? I certainly can't predict. We can never know about the finding. But it's the searching that matters, Custerd. I think that that would be tremendously therapeutic for you."

Tears welled in Custerd's eyes. Hearing Dr. Cilento's words, he immediately knew them to be true. And with their truth came a great shame. How could he have waited so long to do what was so obvious? How long had he taken the easy path, always avoiding the hard way that might have led to happiness? And was it too late now? Was it all his fault? He had tarried. Tarried amongst the comfort of the warm sand and the sunspot in the second bedroom and the fun Boca companions. And all along, Rogo was out there—waiting for him to try.

As if reading these thoughts, Dr. Cilento added, "It's never too late. And it's not your fault. You didn't lose Rogo. But it's your choice now. Face the emptiness you've described to me or try to fill it with something else. But I can tell you from experience. It can't really be filled. It has no bottom."

***

Custerd's voice faded away. A heavy silence filled the room. The dark kept trying to sneak in that window; the yellow lamplight appeared to weaken and tire, dim and blacken. Mr. Rabbit could just about feel how cold the rain must be outside. He was conscious of the noises every bite of his cookie must be making. He told himself it was only loud in his big floppy ears. That his nibbles weren't reverberating outward, breaking whatever spell Custerd's words had cast.

Mr. Rabbit turned his gaze from Custerd to Benny. Benny was utterly still for a long moment following the conclusion of Custerd's tale. Then slowly he reached his paw out, took his first cookie of the night, brought it to his pursed mouth, and took a large deliberate bite. His snout twitched back and forth as he chewed, no other movement in his body. He swallowed. Reached for his tea. Drank in a sip. Swished it around his mouth. Swallowed. Smacked his lips twice. Softly cleared his throat.

"We'll have to see if JFK or LaGuardia is better for flying to Sydney," he said.

Rabbits in the Sky

Mr. Rabbit's pink nose pressed against the cold window of the 747. Just as it had been before—blackness as far as his rabbit eyes could see. He hopped off the armrest and back onto his seat. He turned to ask Benny how long they'd been flying, but he was fast asleep with a blanket wrapped tightly around him. Custerd was asleep too, one more seat over. While Benny's sleep was orderly and calm, Custerd's was the opposite of that. He was inverted in his seat, legs facing the back of the chair. He too lay beneath a blanket, but his was twisted and scattered about so that his left leg and paw were exposed. He wore an orange-and-pink polka-dotted eye mask that he'd packed when he'd left Florida, which, in a feat of engineering, must have been successfully blocking the harsh airplane reading light that shone down directly upon his face. His breath was heavy and periodically punctuated with loud chortles, every chortle accompanied with wriggling of his shoulders and scooting of his hindquarters, even some smacking speech pitched so low as to be utterly incomprehensible.

Mr. Rabbit wondered what he was saying and what he was dreaming to elicit such sleep talking. Knowing what he had learned of Custerd over the last several days as they'd packed up and made arrangements to travel to Australia, the following image flashed through Mr. Rabbit's mind: Custerd dressed in white tie with tails and the full formal accouterments kneeling down in front of a beautiful princess wearing a flowing gown and dazzling tiara, while a crowd of onlookers wearing their Sunday best cheered wildly. The princess was presenting Custerd with a large golden medal for heroic services rendered while he said, "Awww shucks, thanks, princess. You know, if it isn't too much trouble, I'd love some more of that chocolate mousse you had at the palace."

"Maybe I could paint that dream!" thought Mr. Rabbit. But then a cold kind of feeling entered his stomach as he remembered his debut at the gallery. He shook his shoulders and tried to shake the feeling away, let his mind wander down a different path. Reflecting on his time with Custerd thus far, Mr. Rabbit smiled cautiously as he thought of the adventures they'd all had over the last week or so. Custerd had never been to New York City before, so while they made their preparations, they also found time to show Custerd some of the sights around the city. They'd gone to the top of the Empire State Building, gone to see the Statue of Liberty, got lost in the mesmerizing artwork at the Met. But by far and away, Custerd's favorite had been the Museum of Natural History right there in the Upper West Side. He'd stayed for hours amongst the cats of every variety, looking up at them with wide eyes, then trying to imitate their snarling aggressive poses to the best of his ability. It was a little scary for Mr. Rabbit to look at all those giant teeth and razor-sharp claws and wide screaming eyes, but Benny held his hand while they walked around those sections and reminded him that the cats weren't real live cats and that he was completely safe.

A fast friendship had formed between Custerd and Dr. Ursa over his time in New York as well. They shared a mutual love of fish and had gone off on their own for several sushi dinners all about town. One night they'd eaten at Sushi Kaito and gotten so stuffed that they'd taken a taxicab home even though the subway was just two blocks away. Once back in Apartment 1K, Custerd had thrown himself upon the couch and declared Sushi Kaito the finest eating establishment in the world.

"Don't be too hasty," said Dr. Ursa in his soft growl. "I have about five more sushi joints I'm going to take you to when you get back from your adventures down under."

Unfortunately, Dr. Ursa could not join in the trip to search for Rogo. He had patients scheduled at his clinic, and besides, someone needed to watch over things at Apartment 1K. It had been hard getting in the cab and saying goodbye to Dr. Ursa and Pedro, even though Mr. Rabbit knew he'd see them both before long. Both had kindly helped bring the bags out. Pedro had shaken their hands, slapped them on the shoulders, and treated them to that dazzling smile of his. Dr. Ursa had enveloped them all in enormous bear hugs, his voice getting a bit hoarse as he said goodbye. All three adventurers had pressed their faces to the window of the cab as it pulled away from the curb and waved at Dr. Ursa and Pedro, who stood under the awning until the cab was out of sight.

"Well," Mr. Rabbit thought, "everyone's asleep and I am most assuredly not." He slumped back into his seat. A sort of itchy boredom wrinkled through his body. He thought about how he'd like to know what time it was. It was hard to count the hours when you didn't know where to begin. "Maybe I could find Melissa, the very lovely flight attendant who gave us all blankets," he thought. "Besides, it would be oh so good to get out of this chair for a bit and stretch the old feet."

So Mr. Rabbit hopped down from his chair and into the aisle of the plane. He hopped upward toward the galley midway along the plane where he'd last seen Melissa milling about. That was also where some of the bathrooms were. He'd already gone once, and it hadn't been the most pleasant experience. The light was very harsh, and the sudden forceful sucking sound of the toilet flushing was rather intimidating when you were only a seven-inch-tall stuffed rabbit.

When Mr. Rabbit reached the galley, he poked his head around the wall to unobtrusively take a gander. He didn't want to be a bother if Melissa and the other flight attendants were busy, but they all must have rushed off to do something else, because the galley was empty. Disappointed, Mr. Rabbit looked about in the area near the galley, but there was only a girl standing and moving about a bit in the little open spot near the galley and bathroom. Mr. Rabbit hopped over to her.

"Um, hello," said Mr. Rabbit.

"Hello," said the girl.

"You don't happen to know where Melissa, the very kind flight attendant, has gotten to, do you?"

"I'm not sure, but I think all the flight attendants went forward up into the business class cabin for now."

"Oh," said Mr. Rabbit. "I see." He stood there a minute and gave the situation a good think. "Well, it's nice to meet you. I'm Mr. Rabbit." He reached out his paw. The little girl gently took his paw in her hand.

"It's very nice to meet you. I'm Johanna," she said, "but everyone calls me Jo. Except my parents when they're mad at me. Then they call me Miss Johanna Abigail de Quiroz Serrano."

"It's lovely to meet you," said Mr. Rabbit as they shook paw and hand. "Do you happen to know what time it is?"

"Well, it's a little hard to say. You know, because of the time zones. You see, there's the time it is where we began in New York, and then there's the time it is at our destination in Sydney, and then there's the time it is right here, somewhere over the Pacific Ocean."

"Oh," said Mr. Rabbit. He realized his question must have been a little bit silly and that Jo must be quite an intelligent young girl.

"So you're saying that time is different in Australia than it is in New York? And it's also different on this plane?"

"Yes, but that's just the simple way time is different. That's man made. Some old stuffy men, probably with big hairy mustaches, decided that they'd divide up the world and assign different hours to different places so it would make sense when the sun came up and went down. So morning was always in the morning and night was always in the night."

"Oh," said Mr. Rabbit. That made sense, he supposed. While the earth spun around and around, some parts were facing the sun and others were facing away. If it were noon in the place facing the sun, it wouldn't make much sense to call it noon in the place facing away too. Benny had explained something similar to Mr. Rabbit before they had left on their trip. Benny had said that because Australia was in the southern hemisphere, it would be summer when they got there, even though it was winter in New York. It would probably be just as silly to say it was winter in Australia when it was hot and sunny as to say it was noon when it was nighttime.

"But then there's the complicated way time can change," Jo said with a hint of a devilish smile. "There's also Einstein's relativity."

"Oh," said Mr. Rabbit.

"If, for instance, you go very, very fast, then time will move slower for you than for someone not moving at all."

This statement seemed to pull at the edges of Mr. Rabbit's mind in a way that was hot and prickly but also exciting for some unknown reason. A look of concern came into his eyes. He rubbed his chin with his paw.

"Oh …" he said. "Mmmmm, I don't think I really follow that. My good friend Benny the Bunny can hop very, very fast. Are you saying time is slower for him when he hops like that?"

"Well, in a practical sense, no. You have to be going super extraordinarily fast. Like there was an astronaut that lived in a space station circling the earth at high rates of speed for months and when he came back to earth, time had slowed for him, but only by a few microseconds."

"Oh," said Mr. Rabbit.

"I've been very bored and thinking that we are going somewhat fast in this plane and that maybe we are experiencing time just the slightest smidge slower than the people back on the ground."

"That's really a very good thought," said Mr. Rabbit, nodding in approval. "I think about time a lot when I wake up from sleeping. How sometimes when I wake up in the morning I feel like, wow, I got a very nice sleep. It feels like a nice good time has passed. But other times, Dr. Ursa's alarm goes off—Dr. Ursa is my friend—and I think, 'What's this? Where am I? I just fell asleep!' But then it turns out I'd been sleeping for a very long time and it's like I didn't feel the time at all."

"I guess that's another way time can be different. Subjective experience. I read in a book once that a man felt time went by faster when he was happy than when he was unhappy, so he always tried to stay unhappy so his life would last longer. The writer was trying to be silly."

"Oh, that does sound silly," said Mr. Rabbit. Then his fluffy ears perked up. "My friend Benny the Bunny—I think I mentioned him before—he's a writer … but I don't think he writes very many silly things. He writes about mysteries."

"I love mysteries!" said Jo.

"Yeah, me too," said Mr. Rabbit. "I like to be nice and warm and tucked into bed, or a nice spot on the couch, and listen to Benny the Bunny read them to me. It feels very cuddly."

"That does sound very nice," said Jo. Then she paused. "I'm sorry, I realize I never really answered your question. I got too distracted."

"Oh yes, that's right. I did too," said Mr. Rabbit.

Jo looked at her watch, "We've been flying for seven hours. That means we still have thirteen hours to go to Sydney."

"Oh boy," said Mr. Rabbit. "Seven hours in a plane certainly does feel like a very long time. I would say it feels like the happy equivalent would be, mmmmmm … a whole weekend playing in a nice garden with lovely grasses and pretty flowers."

"I agree," said Jo. "You know, it's very important that you make sure you move about and stretch a little when you are on a plane for so very long."

"Um, yeah. Well, I do like to have a good stretch. Should we do some now?"

"Well, yes," said Jo. "That was what I was about to do when you came over and asked about the time."

So Mr. Rabbit and Jo did some stretches together. They reached over and touched their toes. They leaned against the wall of the plane and stretched their calves. Jo showed Mr. Rabbit a good stretch where you sit on the ground and turn your head slightly while pressing lightly with one hand (or paw in Mr. Rabbit's case) against the ground to stretch the area around your neck. It felt very nice to Mr. Rabbit, who realized he'd been a bit stiff in that area. Then Mr. Rabbit showed Jo his favorite yoga stretch where you lay on your back all loosey-goosey and just thought about the breath coming in and out of your body or you thought about not much at all depending on your preference. Jo agreed that it was a very nice stretch indeed.

"Well," Mr. Rabbit said when they had finished doing their stretches, "I guess I better be off to find Melissa the flight attendant. It was very nice playing with you, Jo. Perhaps we can play more later in the flight. I can introduce you to my old pal Benny the Bunny and my new pal Custerd."

"That would be quite lovely," Jo said. So they shook hand and paw again and Mr. Rabbit continued his journey to go see Melissa.

He shimmied his way through the curtain that separated the business-class seats from the economy seats and then started to hop up the aisle. While he was hopping along, it occurred to him that he'd forgotten something, but he couldn't put his paw on what. He paused for a moment midway along the aisle in business class and tried to remember what he had forgotten, but nothing came to him. "Well, if it's important, I'll remember it later," Mr. Rabbit thought and continued to hop along.

When he came to the front of business class, he realized that there was a staircase. "Does this plane have two floors?" he thought. "Wouldn't that just be the bee's knees?" And then he chuckled to himself a bit because he loved that old saying, and every time he said it, he tried to picture what a bee's knees would look like, which always struck his funny bone. "Well, I shouldn't go up those stairs not knowing where they go." But as that thought occurred to him, an even more powerful force entered his mind: "I smell something sweet almost like—carrots. Carrots! Could it be? And they're coming from upstairs." So Mr. Rabbit hopped onto the stairs and began to hop his way upward along the carpeted steps.

Once upstairs, there didn't seem to be very many people. Just the blue glow of TV screens coming from behind some cordoned-off booths. But not far away was a little half-circle bar, with four stools and one lady sitting on one of the stools. "Maybe she knows where the carrots are," Mr. Rabbit thought.

As he closed in on the bar, he became even more certain that the lady would know exactly where the carrots were, because the sweet, earthy smell of the carrots had increased with every hop he'd taken. Reaching the bar, he hopped up onto one of the stools, but he wasn't tall enough to see over the bar or get anyone's attention, so he hopped up onto the bar itself and sat down there.

"Oh!" exclaimed the lady. Then, smiling, "Sorry, you startled me."

"Um, I'm sorry," said Mr. Rabbit, pausing for a moment to bring his paw to his chin before continuing with, "And I'm also Mr. Rabbit. Say, did you happen to smell where that nice carrot smell was coming from?"

The lady laughed, and her laughter was so sudden and sweet it filled Mr. Rabbit with a pleasant warmth in the center of his belly. She had lovely dark hair and was wearing light workout clothes and colorful sneakers that Mr. Rabbit liked very much. "Plus they must be quite practical for staying comfortable on a flight like this," Mr. Rabbit thought. Mr. Rabbit approved of practicality and of very lovely laughter and of carrot smells, so this lady was fast becoming very high in his book.

"My name is Lisa. The carrots are coming from right there." The lady pointed behind the bar, where a man was inserting carrots into some sort of mechanical contraption. "Anthony is making me some fresh carrot juice. Would you like some too?"

"Oh, I would very much like some," said Mr. Rabbit. "I like carrots very much. They are sweet and they are good for your health when eaten in moderation. Well, the moderation part is what my friend Benny the Bunny says. He's very wise about these sorts of things. It can be a bit hard for a stuffed rabbit to be moderate when it comes to carrots … I've had carrot soup and carrot cake and carrot muffins and, you know, just plain carrots, but I've never had carrot juice."

"Anthony," Lisa called to the bartender.

"Yes, ma'am," said Anthony.

"Will you also get my friend here a carrot juice as well? A moderate amount, please."

"Oh, wow!" exclaimed Mr. Rabbit. "I'm really very excited. So, um, why are you going to Australia? I'm going to find a small stuffed lion named Rogo."

"Well, my, that sounds far more interesting than why I'm going," said Lisa. "I suppose I'm going because I never have before and it seemed like a thing to do. Something to cross off the list."

Just then Anthony presented Lisa and Mr. Rabbit with two glasses of bright orange carrot juice—Mr. Rabbit's portion somewhat more moderately sized than Lisa's quite large glass. Still, Mr. Rabbit had to grab the glass with both front paws in order to lift it.

"Well, cheers!" Lisa said, and they clinked their glasses together and Mr. Rabbit had his first sweet sip of fresh carrot juice.

Mr. Rabbit's mouth hung open after he set the glass back down. He scrunched his eyes in surprise; he focused on the taste and feeling that was just now disappearing from his mouth and heading down his throat to his stomach. He looked over at Lisa.

"Like it?" she asked.

"Like it? It's just about the best juice I've ever had. I'm certain I'll never forget drinking my first glass of carrot juice. It's absolutely scrumptious, as my new friend Custerd might say."

"Would you like to tell me about your friends Benny the Bunny and Custerd and about Rogo too?" asked Lisa.

"Absolutely!" said Mr. Rabbit.

***

Just about the same time as Mr. Rabbit was hopping through business class, Benny woke from his sleep in a sudden startled fluster. He'd been dreaming of The Wolf, but what he had dreamed, he couldn't quite say. All that was left in his mind was a fading image tinged in the red of

The Wolf's face, his leering smile and knife-like teeth, his raging eyes, and his insatiable breathing.

Benny shook his head, shook away the dream, and looked over to check on Mr. Rabbit. A sharp absence. "Maybe he's in the bathroom." He looked over at Custerd. His earlier chortles had turned to pure rhythmic snoring.

Benny undid his seatbelt and hopped down onto the floor and out into the aisle. He looked down the aisle at the bathroom indicators on the plane. They all shone green, indicating full vacancy. "Hmmm," thought Benny, a rather unsettled feeling filling his belly. He hopped back up onto his seat, then over to Custerd's seat.

"Custerd," he whispered. "Custerd, have you seen Mr. Rabbit? Do you know where he's gone?"

No response.

Benny sighed and began lightly rocking Custerd's body with his paw.

"Hrrumph!" exclaimed Custerd without opening his eyes. "No, no, not me. Another orange cat ate those." Snoring returned.

Benny rocked Custerd more firmly.

"Huh!" Custerd yelled. "What?" He finally opened his eyes. "Oh! Oh, Benny. Are we there?"

"No. I'm wondering if you know where Mr. Rabbit has gotten to?"

Custerd stretched his arms out wide. Gave his tail a few limbering swipes. Climbed on the armrest and looked over at Mr. Rabbit's empty seat.

"Not the foggiest. Maybe he's making little Mr. Rabbit pellets in the bathroom."

"All the bathrooms are vacant. I better go looking for him." Benny hopped down from the seat and began to leave.

"Hold it, hold it," exclaimed Custerd. "I'll come looking with you, old buddy."

Benny gave Custerd a brief quizzical look and shrugged his shoulders. "OK. Let's try looking around the kitchen galley. Maybe he's trying to see if they have any little treats."

"Well, if he is, he's definitely got the right idea." Custerd had now gotten down from his seat and was slinking his body along next to Benny. "I was just thinking it was about time for a snack."

But Mr. Rabbit was not in the galley. Increasingly worried, Benny hopped up on the back of a sleeping man's seat in the first row of economy class. He looked out over a sea of faces either slack with sleep or glowing in the lights of their entertainment screens. No Mr. Rabbit. He hopped back down.

"Maybe he went to business class," suggested Custerd. "Food's better up there, they say."

***

Jo hadn't been sleeping and she hadn't been watching a movie or TV. She had been thinking. Thinking about the rings around Saturn and how long it would take to ride a spaceship to Titan. And what would the spaceship look like? Would there be vast rooms growing plants to feed the explorers? Would there be spacewalk missions? Would she let go for a moment and just float out there, and in that absolute lightness of floating, would she snatch moments staring out into the pure black of space, like she was the only person in the whole universe, her breath and heart the only noise? Only her, floating alone in a distant sea of blazing stars.

She was lost in these thoughts when she saw a very wise-looking stuffed rabbit hop up onto a seat back in the front of economy. His face seemed a bit pinched. Worried. He hopped back down and joined a stuffed orange cat, who put his arm over the rabbit's shoulders and walked with him through the curtain dividing economy and business class.

"Maybe they're looking for Mr. Rabbit," she thought.

***

When Benny and Custerd entered the business-class cabin, Benny used the same trick to quickly scan the room, only in reverse. He hopped up on the back of a seat at the very back of the cabin and scanned outward. This time it was Benny who was illuminated by a sea of screens. Many of them showed similar images, the viewers at different junctures while watching the same movies or TV shows. A brief thought flashed across Benny's mind: "What unknown similarity connects those watchers who have picked the same entertainment at the same time?" And then, "Is this how I seem when I watch my own shows, like the passengers in this plane, mere receptors for swirling, glowing images?" And then he imagined the image of his own face lit by the glow of the screens like it was lit by the fire of a burning city. And then, "Oh, Mr. Rabbit, where have you gotten yourself to?"

The whispered voice of a girl interrupted Benny's staccato thoughts, which had been thrown from their usual precision by his worry over Mr. Rabbit. The voice said, "Excuse me, sir, but do you happen to be looking for Mr. Rabbit?"

Startled back to reality, Benny just slowly nodded at first, then nodded more emphatically. "Why, yes, I am. Have you seen him?"

"I saw him just a few minutes ago. He told me that he was looking for a flight attendant named Melissa."

"Ah, thanks a hoot, young lady," called Custerd from down in the aisle. "Let's find this Melissa if we can't find that rapscallion rabbit first. Huh, I used to think that Benny was the most rapscallion rabbit in the world, but Mr. Rabbit might be giving him a run for his money these days. I'm Custerd, by the way: champion ice fisher, Boca Raton bon vivant, and a heck of a mahjong player."

Jo introduced herself to Custerd and Benny and all three set off, looking up and down the rows in business class and for the flight attendant Melissa. Suddenly, just as they were swooping past the stairs to the upper deck, Custerd called out, "Hold it!"

"What is it?" asked Jo.

"Do you smell that?" Jo couldn't quite smell what Custerd was talking about, not having the fine olfactory senses of a stuffed rabbit or cat, but Benny did.

"Carrots," Benny said.

"That's right," said Custerd. "And if I were a rapscallion young rabbit out on a looksee for a flight attendant named Melissa, I'd be liable to forget why I was looking for her or that my friends may get worried in my absence if I smelled some real knock-out carrots like these."

Jo and Benny nodded in agreement and the three raced up the stairs, Benny's rapid hops carrying him well ahead of the other two in the group. When he got to the top of the stairs, Benny sighed a great sigh of relief. There was Mr. Rabbit sitting on top of a bar sipping a drink and chatting with a beautiful dark-haired woman. Arriving at his side, Custerd lightly elbowed Benny and indicated the woman with a flip of his orange head. "Rrrrrowl," he said in a light growl, Custerd's traditional acknowledgment of feminine beauty.

Now with far less haste, the group made their way over to the bar. As they arrived, the woman had to tap Mr. Rabbit on the shoulder so that he would realize his friends had arrived, so lost was he in telling the story of Benny rescuing him from his wild ride on the back of Felix the dog.

"Oh!" exclaimed Mr. Rabbit. "It's all my pals. And even my newest pal Jo. Well, second newest. Lisa's my newest pal."

Benny hopped up on the bar and gave Mr. Rabbit a tight squeeze. Custerd crawled his way onto one of the barstools and had Jo lift him up onto the bar as well. He gave Mr. Rabbit an affectionate tousling of his head fur, then introduced himself to Lisa as "Custerd: regional over-40 feline ping-pong champion, finder of stuffed rabbits, and connoisseur of both confectionaries and feminine wiles."

There was great relief all around that Mr. Rabbit was found and had managed to meet such a nice young woman and try his first taste of fresh carrot juice. Letting down his fur a bit after his worried searching, Benny decided to indulge in a little carrot juice himself. Custerd ordered a hot chocolate and inspired Jo to do the same. They all had a pleasant chat there at the bar, getting to know each other a bit more, and passed an enjoyable hour of a long flight.

When they had all made their way back to their seats, Mr. Rabbit felt very cozy as he tucked himself into his blanket. He thought about the carrot juice that filled his belly. He thought about the nice people he was already meeting on his journey. He thought about how much Benny and Custerd loved him that they got so worried about him and how much he loved them in turn. And as he thought these things, he fell fast asleep and didn't wake until breakfast was served, two hours or so before landing in Sydney.

THE DOWN-UNDER CLUB

Mr. Rabbit thought Sydney must be just about the most beautiful city in the world. He pressed his face against the window again as they made their descent. The sparkling blue waters. The curving white opera house. The glistening clean lines of the office buildings. He was so excited to get out and explore, the long journey fairly melted away, and he was bursting with energy as the three adventurers made their way off the plane and into the customs line.

Getting through customs proved to be a snafu, though. When their turn was called, the three stuffed animals made their way up to a middle-aged man with wispy blond hair and leathery skin sitting at a desk. Benny the Bunny handed the man each of their passports, Benny having been deemed most reliable to look after such important documents. The wispy blond man took the passports without saying anything, rifled through the pages a few moments, looked up, and pointed to Custerd. "OK, you're fine to go through." Then he looked at Mr. Rabbit and Benny the Bunny. "You two are denied entry. No rabbits allowed in Australia. Invasive species."

"No rabbits!" exclaimed Mr. Rabbit with a look of horror.

"That's right," said the wispy blond man.

The stuffed animals began to argue with the man, but he would hear nothing of it. Fortunately, Jo was in the customs line with her parents, not far behind. "Oh no!" she thought. "They're in trouble!" She pulled away from her parents, who, dazed from the flight, didn't react until she was well on her way. "Jo!" her mom yelled. "Where are you going!" but Jo didn't turn around. She knew just what she needed to do, for she had spotted the somehow-perfectly-elegant-after-such-a-long-flight Lisa talking to her own customs agent.

Panting a bit with her burst of running after sitting so long, Jo called out to Lisa, "The guys—they're not letting them through, Lisa. They say they're rabbits so they can't come into Australia." Now, Lisa had been having an entirely lovely chat with her customs official, who was even recommending to her some off-the-beaten-path sights to see around the city.

"Not being allowed in!" she exclaimed. "All of the guys?"

"Well, just the rabbits," Jo explained. "Says they're an 'invasive species.'"

"How can this be, Aiden?" Lisa asked her customs official.

"Well, that's right. We don't allow rabbits into Australia."

"But these are no simple rabbits. They're stuffed animal rabbits," Lisa explained.

"Hmmm, well, I suppose that's fine," said Aiden. "Hey, I'll tell you what. Let's go explain things to Bill. He can be a bit of a stickler for the rules."

So Aiden and the two girls marched over to where an increasingly flustered and worried Benny the Bunny argued with wispy blond-haired Bill the customs official.

"What's this all about, then, Bill?" asked Aiden.

"Some rabbits trying to get into Australia. Can't you see?"

"But those aren't regular rabbits. Those are stuffed animal rabbits," explained Aiden with a chorus of "yeahs!" from Lisa and Jo.

"Don't matter what kind of rabbit they are," said Bill. But hearing Aiden coming to their defense gave Benny the Bunny an idea.

"Well, actually, sir, perhaps it does matter. You see, technically we're not really a type of rabbit. We are a type of wawa. You see, a rabbit is from the Leporidea family of the Lagomorpha order of mammal, of which there are several species, such as the *Sylvilagus floridanus*—colloquially known as the Eastern cottontail. However, Mr. Rabbit and myself, while sharing a deep affinity and spiritual connection to our rabbit brethren, are actually the same species as our friend Custerd here. We are all *Wawa sapiens*. You might say, in our hearts, we are rabbits. On our surface, we are not. So how will you judge us? By our surface or our hearts? By neither? By both?"

Now Bill became a bit flummoxed.

"Well, that's all well and good, but ..." Bill noticed the eyes of Mr. Rabbit and Benny the Bunny staring up at him. He noticed Jo and Lisa and Aiden and Custerd looking at him. He looked out more broadly at what seemed to be the entire plane full of people staring at him with looks of concern and mild disgust. "But—but—but—I suppose everything is in order, then. Welcome to Australia."

"Thanks, Bill!" Mr. Rabbit called out in excitement, and smiles lit up Jo and Lisa's faces.

When they'd all passed through the customs counter, Benny the Bunny rigorously shook Jo and Lisa's hands. "I can't thank you fine ladies enough. You really came to our rescue there."

"Hohoho, yes indeed," Custerd joined in. "I think Benny here was just about to plotz when you came over."

"Plotz?" asked Lisa.

"It's Yiddish," answered Jo. "It's like verklempt."

"Verklempt?" asked Lisa.

"Overcome with emotion," said Benny the Bunny.

"Oh, I see," said Lisa.

By this point they were all walking together through the airport out toward the taxicab stand and warm Sydney air.

"Hohoho, yeah," Custerd interjected. "When I was getting sushi with our pal Dr. Ursa, he told me that Mr. Rabbit here met Rabbi Greenberg at a building mixer and the rabbi said, 'Hi, I'm the rabbi,' and Mr. Rabbit says, 'Well, hello. I guess I'm the rabb*it. Mr. Rabbit*, to be precise.' Hohoho!"

"Well, if there's anything I can do to help you darling gentlemen, you just let me know," offered Lisa with a big smile on her face. "In fact, I insist on it. There's just something about you fellas …" And she shook her head, not knowing how to put her finger on how she felt about her blossoming friendship with the wawas.

It had been a struggle for Lisa recently. She'd been in a relationship for a long time that had ended. Her friends had mostly moved out of New York and to the suburbs. And those that were left in the city … she felt as though their interests were diverging. That they were never on the same page; that their pursuits and concerns left her cold and bored. She felt stuck. But she also felt a renewed strength. She knew that in order to get unstuck, she had to do it for herself. So she was taking a grand tour of the world and starting with Australia, the farthest place from New York that she could think of. And already, not even out of the airport doors, she'd made new friends who were warm and generous of spirit.

"Me too!" called Jo. So they all exchanged information on where they were staying and their itinerary in Australia. The first part would be easy enough—it turned out that they were all staying at the same hotel in Sydney, the Park Hyatt.

"See, guys," Custerd explained. "Your old buddy knows how to pick a hotel. Everybody's doing it!" And even Benny the Bunny was now glad they were staying there, despite having almost fainted when Custerd first showed him the nightly room rate.

***

The first night in Sydney, the wawas focused mostly on getting some sleep and getting over their jet lag. After such a long flight and the change in time that Mr. Rabbit had learned all about from Jo, a stuffed rabbit or cat could become quite disoriented and needed to take it easy for a little bit. So that's just what the wawas did. They slept and ate and took little walks and made sure to stretch until they began to feel themselves again.

The next afternoon, though, they were ready to begin their adventure. The obvious first stop was the University of Sydney, where Rogo had last been seen.

The university was full of majestic castle-like buildings. The wawas wandered through the main green, looking upward in awe and dislocation. It was as if on seeing the grand antiquity of the buildings around them, the enormity of their task finally dawned on them. They had to find a small stuffed lion that had been missing for twenty-five years in an enormous world, and all they had to go on was that he was last seen amongst these rambling castles, bundled up in bed sheets.

Remembering the bed sheets, the guys shook out the daze that threatened to overwhelm their fuzzy heads and asked for directions to the university laundry room. Walking among the industrial-sized washing machines, Mr. Rabbit felt as overwhelmed as he had outside amongst the castles.

A sea of gigantic white washers threw sheets in a steady circle. Up, over, down, over, up, over, down, over. Mr. Rabbit became lost staring at the endless rhythm. It seemed as if *he* were trapped in the washer. That *he* was being thrown in an endless loop. Up, over, down, over, up, over, down, over.

"Snap out of it, lop ear!" bawled Custerd. "I swear you're ready to get hypnotized at the drop of a hat." Then, reflecting on how he himself had been hypnotized by the waves and the crab at the beach in Boca, he added, "Well, I suppose I've been down that road myself ... but not while on a mission of vast import!"

73

"Oh, sorry, Custerd," replied Mr. Rabbit. "I suppose it's all a bit much, you know? I mean, just the size of these washers themselves. It's like they have no personality. No hominess to them. Not like our washer in Apartment 1K at all. It would be a terrible thing to be lost in one of these. Like falling into a black hole. How long would you be there just cycling about until you were finally snatched out by accident? Would you remember yourself when you finally escaped or would you be some new creature? Is this really what Rogo went through? And then afterward … *no finding*. No comfort at the end of a harrowing journey. Only solitude. Where could he have gone from here?"

The guys were solemn and silent a moment, feeling that Mr. Rabbit had made into words exactly what they were all feeling on the inside. Custerd and Benny had experienced Rogo's loss in terms of what it had meant to them. The loss of a friend. A hole in their heart. But now, for the first time they were forced to confront what becoming lost must have felt like to Rogo himself. They thought of all the times they had been scared and been comforted in their fright. About all the times they had felt lost but then swiftly found. Then they imagined what it would be like to be scared and lost, but then … "no finding," as Mr. Rabbit had put it. Benny the Bunny imagined falling into The Wolf's open maw and all turning to black. Custerd imagined taking some false step off a great height and tumbling in the air forever. And Mr. Rabbit just stared at the cycling load of sheets and imagined never meeting Benny the Bunny and his heart perpetually waiting at the precipice of hopeful finding with no end in sight. Alone without a friend.

After a while, there was nothing to be found in the laundry room, and the guys drifted out of the room and its heat and endlessly repeating noise. They wandered back outside onto the green amongst the castles and sat together on a bench, their paws listlessly swinging in the open air. And, hardly speaking, they sat there until the sun began to set, each thinking their own lonely thoughts.

As the colors of the sunset began to darken and blacken, as the air turned cold and still they knew not what to do, it was in that moment, without any fanfare, that a two-foot-tall stuffed kangaroo hopped by their bench without taking the slightest notice of them.

So deep was the guys' stupor, the kangaroo almost failed to register. But Custerd managed to process the implications of his vision before the kangaroo was completely out of sight. "Hohoho, everyone!" he cried. "That was a wawa kangaroo! A wawa! And on his own like us. We've got to ask him about Rogo!"

And as if slapped awake, the rabbits shook themselves alert with hardy oh yeses, and they all scrambled after the kangaroo shouting out, "Good sir!" and "Pardon me!"

Eventually the kangaroo heard the shouts, paused his hopping, and turned to look at the guys. "G'day! What can I do you for?"

Custerd was too out of breath to speak, so it was Benny the Bunny who took the lead. "Good evening, sir. Very sorry to bother you. We've come to Australia to search for an old friend of ours who was left here. We were wondering if you might have any advice as to how to begin. We only know that he was left at this university and that he was scooped up in the bed sheets and never heard from again."

"Right. Well, that's how it happens, isn't it?" replied the kangaroo.

"Pardon me?" asked Benny the Bunny.

"Well, it's a uni. Kids come in with a stuffy, one reason or another, the stuffy goes missing. Heck, that's how I got here. How all of us got here."

"All of us?" asked Benny.

"Yeah, we've got a whole crew. A kind of club. I was just heading there now for a pint. You're welcome to come along if you'd like to check the place out."

So Custerd and the rabbits found themselves making their way across campus with the kangaroo. They all got to chatting and they learned a bit more about their new companion. His name was Joel, although apparently the intention was to name him Joey. "A bit generic, if you ask me," but, as is often the case, his human struggled a bit with the pronunciation, and after being Joe-Wa for a good while, he eventually settled on Joel. "Still consider Joe-Wa my formal name, mind you. But Joel's good enough when knocking about."

"Know what you mean," Custerd had replied, nodding. "My formal name is Custerd Custerdberg 'El Custardo' von und zu Custopia, His Majestic High-Catness, Emperor Extraordinaire of the Universe. But I usually humbly shorten it to Custerd."

Eventually Joel led the crew to a small door in the side of the main castle-like university building. A rabbit had to hop down into a hollowed-out portion of the ground to notice the door if you didn't know where to look. "I'd worry about the drainage in a storm," thought Benny the Bunny. But once a rabbit hopped down into the depression, the door was a rather solid dark wood standing about four and a half feet high.

Joel gave a quick knock on the door and a small metal slot in the center of the door that Benny had assumed was used for mail flipped open, revealing glistening eyes.

"Password," the eyes appeared to say.

"Galloping gorilla," replied Joel.

"Password," the eyes said again.

"I just told you, didn't I?"

A long sigh. "No, Joel, that was the password last month. Don't you remember we changed it last meeting?"

"Oh, right. Yeah, I remember now. What was the new one again?"

"Salivating salamander."

"Oh, that's right. Well, salivating salamander, then."

And, with the magic words being spoken, the door opened inward and a rather formal-looking wawa panda was revealed. He was dressed in a three-piece Donegal tweed with a regimental striped tie. He had small wire-rimmed spectacles sitting about halfway down his snout, and he looked through those spectacles with disapproval at Joel, Custerd, and the rabbits. Then, with a snort of put-upon acceptance, he began to lead everyone down a dark wood-paneled hallway.

As he walked along the hall, Mr. Rabbit looked at the pictures that hung upon the walls. Each contained a portrait of a rather dignified-looking wawa. There was a monocle-wearing crocodile, a monkey sporting tennis whites, a polar bear in a double-breasted tuxedo, a pig in a deep green evening gown, a frog doffing a bowler, and a cow wearing a finely tailored shark-skin suit.

Looking back and seeing Mr. Rabbit staring up at the pictures in awe, the tweed-wearing panda proclaimed, "You'll notice portraits of our past club presidents. Members in good standing cast votes. A simple plurality selects the winner. The term is one annum. A past president must wait five years before becoming eligible again." The panda pointed to a second portrait of the monocle-wearing crocodile. "Most impressively, Carlos Crocodile here has served four terms as club president. Quite a feat of endurance, administrative stewardship, and political acumen ..."

As the panda was talking, he entered a vast room that took Mr. Rabbit's breath away. Two walls were dark wood as in the hallway, but the other two were entirely bookshelves. A fire crackled in a grand fireplace at the opposite end of the room. Throughout the space were small tables surrounded by three or four upholstered chairs. In most of the chairs sat wawas of all sorts—drinking tea or coffee, reading newspapers or books, chatting with their fellow members, or, in the case of one blue-blazer-wearing gorilla, soundly napping. There was a pair of billiards tables, and the cow from one of the portraits Mr. Rabbit had noted in the hall struck a relaxed pose leaning against the side of one of the tables while a platypus focused furiously on his next shot.

"... gentlemen," continued the panda, "welcome to The Down-Under Club."

"Wow," said Mr. Rabbit.

"Indeed," replied the panda.

"Now this is what I'm talking about!" Custerd exclaimed. "A cat could get used to this. You guys serving some supper soon? Maybe some finger sandwiches? Like the kind with the crust cut off? We could skip straight to dessert if we missed the main event. I don't think you'd hear any of us complain. I bet you've got some cakes around somewhere. Maybe a pudding or tart or something of that sort? Or just something chocolate. Anything chocolate would do."

"May I inquire after your reason for gracing us at The Down-Under Club?" asked the panda, ignoring Custerd's food-related line of questioning.

"We're looking for a small wawa lion by the name of Rogo," Benny the Bunny interjected. "All we know is that he was lost here at the university about twenty-five years ago. Joel here was kind enough to bring us to The Down-Under Club in hopes that Rogo might have passed through here or perhaps someone here knows something about him."

"Rogo, Rogo, Rogo ... hmmmm, don't know the name ..." began the panda.

"I was hoping we might talk to some of the longer-serving patrons. Carlos Crocodile, for instance. Your description of his terms as club president implied to me that he might have been around at the time."

"Well, I'll tell you all what. There's a social hour coming up in ..." the panda shook out an elegant evening watch that had been hidden under his tweed jacket, "thirty-five minutes. I'll arrange for some chairs for you and a spot of tea, if you're so inclined. The social hour would be a good time to approach without disturbing the members from their reading or ..." he loosely gesticulated toward the soundly sleeping gorilla, "whatever reverie they currently find themselves in."

As the panda seemed to be finishing his statement, Custerd started to interject, only to be cut off by a hastily raised panda paw and a strained "Annnnd ..." so that all Custerd managed to get out was a high-pitched squeak. "After the social hour," the panda continued, turning toward Custerd, "there will indeed be a light supper served if you all have no other pressing arrangements."

"IPPP ..." Another high-pitched squeak as Custerd was cut off again, almost at the exact moment he began to draw breath to speak. "AND ..." the panda began again, "dessert will indeed be on offer. And ..." This time Custerd had no chance to even begin to intervene. "Yes, there will be some small biscuits and what-not available to accompany the tea."

"Well, hot paws on asphalt!" Custerd cried, finally managing to get a word in. "What more could a cat ask for? Hey, say, panda, you don't happen to have a branch of this club up in Boca, do ya?"

"I'm aware of no such institution. The Down-Under Club is itself modeled after the venerable Ulysses Club in London. Other than the two, I'm not aware of any others. Although if in your travels you do come across another club and it seems to meet our standards, we'd appreciate it if you informed us of it. We're always interested in forming reciprocal relationships with fellow clubs for when our members travel abroad."

"Thank you so much, Sir Panda. I do apologize, but in all the excitement we failed to ask your name?" asked Benny the Bunny.

"My name is Chauncey Panda. A pleasure."

All the wawas chatted a bit more as Chauncey Panda led them to four overstuffed upholstered chairs, Joel having decided to join them. Tea was soon served, and Custerd made do with some small, rather plain, only slightly sweet wheat biscuits.

The more they all chatted with Joel, the more impressed Mr. Rabbit became. He couldn't imagine anyone leading a life as adventurous as Joel's. The kangaroo told them all about the outback. He told them about how Carlos Crocodile was a congenial sort, but a real crocodile was a dangerous proposition, especially if it were just you alone with your wits and your knife and high-hopping kangaroo legs to help you out of the situation. That part put a notion in Mr. Rabbit's head. How both rabbits and kangaroos had very powerful hind legs to hop along with. Following that thought, Mr. Rabbit began to think that perhaps there was a deep connection between himself, Benny the Bunny, all sorts of rabbits, even, and the high-hopping marsupials of Australia. "Maybe I was always meant to come here," he thought. "Strange how so many chances have brought me to this moment, yet it seems like I'm right where I ought to be—need to be, even."

Just as Chauncey Panda had said, precisely thirty-five minutes after they'd sat down for tea, a small bell was struck. Hearing its clear, sharp sound, all the wawas began to roust themselves, some stretching a bit and letting out deeply satisfied sighs, and before long, a sizeable crew of wawas were milling about the room for social hour. It was then that Benny the Bunny spotted the monocle-wearing Carlos Crocodile emerging from a side room with a folded newspaper tucked under one arm.

"Excuse me, Carlos Crocodile," Benny the Bunny said. "My friends and I were hoping to ask you a question."

"Oh. Oh, certainly. Are you looking to apply for membership?" replied Carlos Crocodile, somewhat startled to be so quickly accosted as social hour began, and by so novel a group.

"Well, we're here to try to find an old lion named Rogo …" began Benny the Bunny, but Custerd, in his eagerness, was having trouble letting Benny the Bunny take the lead.

"That's right! A sweet wawa lion named Rogo. He's really handsome and quite petite. And he likes to run around like this." Custerd got down on all fours and began to do a slow imitation of Rogo running, launching off both back feet and landing gracefully on both front paws before launching off the back ones again. Custerd did this in a circle around Carlos Crocodile, who appeared thoroughly overwhelmed by the stimulation. Benny was struck almost dumb by the accuracy of Custerd's imitation of Rogo. How had he remembered that so precisely?

Benny rubbed at his right eye with his right paw, gave his head a little shake, and began again.

"He would have been here maybe a long time ago. As long as twenty-five years ago. We were hoping that since you've been a member here so long, you might remember him if he ever passed through the club. Perhaps remember where he'd gone from here?"

As Benny spoke, Carlos continued to watch Custerd's slow imitation of Rogo running as if hypnotized. Benny's words registered somewhere in his mind, but it was like he could not tear himself away from watching Custerd's undulating orange movements.

Finally, Custerd stopped, looked up at the crocodile, and said, "So whatcha think, partner? You know this lion?"

Carlos Crocodile started to respond, but what came out was a long, stuttering pause where he appeared to review, revise, correct, amend, and modify what he was about to say several times without actually saying anything.

Mr. Rabbit and the rest of the guys waited on the crocodile with bated breath. Even Joel seemed to have been caught up in the drama of the moment. Finally, sounds began to solidify in Carlos's mouth, and the gang collectively leaned closer, their mouths hanging a bit open.

"Without getting your hopes up, I believe I do know the lion you speak of. It was many years ago. I hadn't even served my first term as club president yet. The more I think about it, the clearer the image becomes. We were all sat around just like today—the club members, I mean—when Calypso Pig, who worked the door in those days, brought a small lion into the room covered in a blanket. The lion was all wet, you see. Soaking, really. And very shaken. Sad to say, but whether soaking or not, that's how many of us are when we first seek membership. Shaken to the core. Lost.

"His name was Rogo. That sounds right. It's been so many years it's hard to really say for sure. But hearing you say the name, it hits my ear in a manner too familiar to be altogether new.

"We took Rogo in, of course. Helped him dry off. Got him a cup of tea. Got some food in him. If I remember correctly, he'd been thrown in a washing machine ..."

"That's him!" cried Custerd, unable to contain his excitement.

"What happened after that?" asked Benny the Bunny.

"He stayed for a period of time. I had a couple of nice conversations with him, as I recall. A very amiable young lion. But not everyone is made out for club life. Certain wawas feel the need to move on. To go off on their own. I have the faintest recollection ... of a small lion talking to a koala at social hour just like we're having now. The small lion—Rogo, I imagine—was saying that he hadn't been abandoned, that he'd just been lost. That he needed to find a way back home. And I think I remember, well, because it struck me as so strange, because the koala suggested Rogo take a walkabout."

"A walkabout?" asked Mr. Rabbit.

"An old aboriginal tradition that we Australian wawas have adopted and modified as our own. The aboriginals would go walkabout when they came of age. Going off on their own into the wild for a time, wandering and living by themselves. Some Australian wawas perform a similar ritual when their humans move on and they must learn to live on their own. They go walkabout to find who they are without their humans. I think the koala ... I wish I could remember the koala's name ... was telling Rogo that maybe that would help him find some direction, help lead him back to where he'd come from."

"Wow!" exclaimed Mr. Rabbit.

"By any chance, do you know where he would have gone walkabout?" Benny asked.

"I do," interjected Joel, everyone turning to him in anticipation.

"Well, I assume I do. Most wawas go walkabout—well, we kangaroos call it hop-about—anyways, most wawas go walkabout—or hop-about or prowl-about as the case may be—up over the mountains in a particularly wild part of the outback we wawas call the Down-Under Waste. Not sure what the humans call it. I'm guessing if Rogo went hop-about, that's likely where he went."

"Well, that settles it!" cried Custerd. "We've got to go hop-about! When do we start? I mean, right away, right? Right away; right after dessert."

"You'll need supplies. And you'll need a guide," replied Joel.

"Yes, of course … we'll need … we'll need …" murmured Benny the Bunny, starting to think through all of the practicalities and contingencies of their next adventure.

"Where can we find a guide?" asked Mr. Rabbit.

"Right in front of you, of course," said Joel. "Been meaning to stretch the old legs anyways."

HOP-ABOUT, PART I

The vastness of it. So much of the outback stunned Mr. Rabbit, but that's what he kept coming back to. Who knew there were lands like this, lands that stretched on and on seemingly forever? And this just one part of one country. One country in one world in one solar system in one galaxy out of who knew how many galaxies.

The sheer vastness of it all.

The Down-Under Waste made Mr. Rabbit feel very small. And at night, with no human light around for untold miles, the stars shown like brilliant diamonds you could reach out and touch. The first night, while hopping out of the tent to do his necessaries, and the fire already smothered and cold, he had yelped in fear of the stars, they'd seemed so close and bright.

And the walking. Never had he done so much walking. Sometimes the heat in the day was so much that he felt as though all his fur had puffed out and then sagged in exhaustion along with his arms and feet. And though they'd start most days at a hopping pace (Custerd hustling along as best he could, lightly grousing and complaining at first, then becoming too tired even for that), by the time they would rest, it was all that Mr. Rabbit could do to let his head hang and watch one lovely furry foot take one more step and stop, then to somehow force the other foot to follow suit with yet one more.

Joel had them well provisioned. While hopping or walking, Mr. Rabbit often thought about their last night in the hotel. Joel had shown up at their room with what seemed like a dragon's hoard of supplies. Food supplies. Cooking supplies. Medical supplies. Camping supplies. And old square German-style structured backpacks for them to carry it all.

Then they'd gone down and had a wonderful time with Lisa and Jo in the lobby. They'd drank tea with milk and honey and had tried to eat vegemite sandwiches, which no one could stomach except for Lisa, who said she almost perversely enjoyed it. They'd laughed and told stories. Lisa and Jo had talked about the places they'd visited in Sydney and where they were going next. And they had listened in fascination to the wawas about the adventure they were about to embark on.

And gloriously, all throughout the lobby, there had been air conditioning. Mr. Rabbit never knew he could miss something so much that he had barely noticed operating in the background. When he got back to Apartment 1K, he was going to find the window unit that cooled the master bedroom at night and give it a big hug, a hearty pat, and a sincere thank you.

Joel had explained that once they had made their way by bus to the Down-Under Waste, that they must proceed by foot to make it a true hop-about. That after twenty-five years, there was no logical way to track Rogo. No straight path to their destination. Instead, they needed to trust in the land, trust it to guide them. Joel warned that the land and its spirits were not there for their whims, that it might take them to some destination of its own for what seemed its own purposes, but all they could do was trust. Trust that their sprits would grow within themselves and that the land would be kind if their hearts were open and their minds were clear.

And to have clear minds and open hearts, they had to hop and they had to walk. They had to become a part of the land and the trees and the rivers (which Joel called billabongs). To connect with the life of the Down-Under Waste. And to some extent to leave themselves behind, or at least the self they thought they knew. To, as Joel had described it, "awaken to the world and to yourself. To all of yourself, even the parts you keep hidden away or the parts that you never knew you had."

It made Mr. Rabbit think of his painting. How when he painted it was as if he floated on some current of self that didn't speak words, let alone make philosophical arguments, but instead simply moved him to one brush stroke, to one color, to one image, and then the next and the next until the spell broke or faded. When he imagined "awakening" to that part of him ... it wasn't fear exactly ... he wasn't quite sure how to think of it. All that seemed to come to him was an image of him climbing up on top of the stones of some old well, then leaning out over the edge and looking down into the well water, the water perfectly still and perfectly deep. Deep without bottom, so that although the water was perfectly clear, as you looked down into its depths, it paradoxically became perfectly dark and black. Mr. Rabbit could imagine leaning over and taking a pawful of that water and drinking. It made him nervous, but he could even imagine floating on the water's surface ... but diving down into the depths ... when he thought of that, it was like his mind came up against a perfect black wall, impenetrable and smooth and racing off forever in every direction. To even think of pushing against it with one furry paw made his heart and stomach feel as if they were sinking without end. And Mr. Rabbit thought at first, "How will I ever learn who I am with this black wall?" But shortly following upon that thought, ever the optimist, he realized, "Well at least I know about the wall now."

Some of the land had been as he imagined. Red, gravelly ground. Low-slung green bushes. Some was lusher, bright trees and dazzling rivers (or billabongs). Joel said, "Watch out for the snakes." And Joel also said, "If you don't bother them, they won't bother you ... most likely." So Mr. Rabbit would whisper as he went, "It's OK, snakes, just passing through. No need to worry or fuss."

Some of the land was as he imagined, but some was not. The places where the fires had come—those parts had turned black and dead. When Mr. Rabbit walked through forests of black and ashen trees, black soot underneath, he felt as if he walked through a scary story come to life. And when he walked where there had been few trees, mostly only bush that had burned away, he felt as if he walked along a red moon.

One evening, after they had finally passed through a long stretch in the part Mr. Rabbit thought of as the red moon, the wawas, with great relief, entered into a green forest. Then, upon finding a beautiful river with trees bending and hanging out over its swooping curves and water sparkling purple and red in the sunset, the wawas made camp.

They hustled out to scavenge up some vegetables from the forest. Mr. Rabbit was lucky to find a patch of beetroot to bring back for everyone. Custard returned sadly dragging some stalks of celery, but then brightened when he saw that Benny the Bunny had found a great haul of mushrooms. "Oh boy!" Custard yelled out after giving the mushrooms a good sniff. "I feel like I'm dining at the Ritz!"

Joel cooked up the food over the fire. The whole crew ate and smiled, even though they were all worn down at this point, their fur unwashed and covered in soot and red stained. Mr. Rabbit thought that they could all use a nice morning swim in the river before they headed out tomorrow. Benny the Bunny and Custerd even laughed a bit as they told an old story from when they'd lived in Massachusetts together in that old house near the woods. They had organized a great football game between all the wawas in the neighborhood. Despite Benny's superior knowledge of the game's strategy and tactics, Custerd had won easily, Benny's team not scoring a single touchdown, because Custerd had recruited to anchor his line a gigantic red dog wawa named Ralph that a neighbor kid's father had won in a carnival game.

After dinner, the sunset colors were long fled from the sky, and a pure blackness, a kind of which Mr. Rabbit had hardly seen in his life, settled in at their makeshift camp's edge. The light from the campfire cast the dark back, but it seemed to hang about the camp like a living thing. Mr. Rabbit shivered thinking of things out in that dark. And not just of the things in the dark, he realized, but of *the dark itself.*

Joel took out an instrument that Mr. Rabbit hadn't realized he'd brought with him. It looked like a long hollow stick, and on the sides it was adorned with fantastic colored carvings of kangaroos. Joel explained it was called a didgeridoo and passed it around so that everyone could take a look. When it got back to him, Joel took the didgeridoo up to his lips and began to blow through his mouth, moving his cheeks in a strange puffing beat.

The sounds were different from anything Mr. Rabbit had ever heard. Completely and utterly foreign. But something in the sounds … there was something of the first things in the sounds. As if upon first hearing they immediately became fully familiar. Like long-lost relatives. Primordial and essential. Mr. Rabbit felt as if he were hearing the recesses of his mind, the hidden rhythm of his life made sound. He felt grounded to the land. To the river. To the forest. As if the sounds made distance disappear and he floated along a different kind of river. A river of stars. Of lives. Of heartbeats. Of bravery and cowardice. Of malice and kindness. And always a reaching out. A grasping at hands. Of connection and oneness. That the hands you grasped were your own.

The noise of the didgeridoo faded. And as that powerful sound echoed away, Mr. Rabbit could hear the slightest noises at the camp's edge. A soft rustling.

Putting away the instrument, Joel began to sing out in a voice pure, high, and sweet. Wholly transfigured from his speaking voice. He sang out:

Once a jolly swagman camped by a billabong
Under the shade of a coolibah tree
He sang as he watched and waited till his billy boiled
You'll come a-Waltzing Matilda, with me

Waltzing Matilda, Waltzing Matilda
You'll come a-Waltzing Matilda, with me ...

And with the shock of that beautiful noise that sang out from within Joel, Mr. Rabbit was transfixed. The words seemed to play upon his heart. Like his heart had become the instrument that vibrated with this holy sound. And mixed with that sacred, sweet voice came a background murmur of the meandering river and of the rustling growing louder at the edges of the firelight.

Up rode the squatter, mounted on his thoroughbred
Up rode the troopers, one, two, three
With the jolly jumbuck you've got in your tucker bag
You'll come a-Waltzing Matilda, with me

Waltzing Matilda, Waltzing Matilda
You'll come a-Waltzing Matilda, with me ...

The sounds of the rustling grew and grew as Joel sang. The rustling almost seemed to become a beat in time to Joel's voice. Thrumming through the camp as a thing physically felt, as if the sound were an electric current.

Up jumped the swagman and sprang into the billabong
You'll never catch me alive, said he ...

That's when Mr. Rabbit saw the first of them. A koala. Not a wawa, but a wild koala. His big eyes glowed in the light. There was a nobility to his injured walk. A dignity, like an old man dressed in an evening suit, walking tall with a shining black cane.

And his ghost may be heard as you pass by that billabong
You'll come a-Waltzing Matilda, with me …

Then there were others. Kangaroos and wallabies. Furry wombats waddling. More koalas too. Even a cadre of field mice. And many carried wounds with them. Many had been touched by fire. Scars upon their flesh or in their hearts. And as Joel came to the last verse, their voices rose up and sang in chorus with him.

Waltzing Matilda, Waltzing Matilda
You'll come a-Waltzing Matilda, with me
His ghost may be heard as you pass by that billabong
You'll come a-Waltzing Matilda, with me.

A deep silence followed, as if the entire wood were hushed. Mr. Rabbit felt something below his eyes. He raised his paw to it and felt the wetness that matted his fur there. It was only then that he realized he'd been crying. He looked over at Benny and Custerd and saw that they were crying too, Benny quietly and Custerd with big heaving intakes of breath.

"Why is it so sad?" Mr. Rabbit asked Benny the Bunny after a while.

Benny paused a long moment. Then he spoke, quietly and unusually haltingly at first.

"Because it's about things lost. Lost ways of life. Lost places and people and ideas. We are lucky in our lives for the new things that come and the things that endure. And we are lucky to remember the things lost too. But only we who remember can carry those things. And with so few hands put to the work of carrying, they lay heavy in our hearts."

HOP-ABOUT, PART II

The more time he spent with koalas, the more Custerd discovered—he dug their vibe.

Last night had been quite an evening. Quite an evening indeed. After all of the animals had revealed themselves and they'd all had a good cry and the huggers had hugged and the hand-shakers had shaken hands, they'd stayed up late into the wee hours of the morning talking about anything and everything. About all the animals had been through, about the land, the river, the forest, about whispered rumors of the valley over yonder. And the wawas had told their tale too, of their hop-about and their search for Rogo.

It had been a lot to take in. So much so that Custerd had dug into his dwindling reserve of dark chocolate Hershey bars and taken a couple of surreptitious nibbles to calm his nerves and excitement.

They'd all slept till noon, which was just as well—no need to endure the heat of the day. So they'd eaten a late breakfast, which, with the animals' help, turned out to be quite a bounty of vegetables from the forest. Still, it wasn't what Custerd was used to. And after all the time out prowling the Down-Under Waste, Custerd thought wistfully of his old life (the rabbits might call it a hop-about, but he always thought of it as a prowl-about—really, a good prowl should be slow and slinky, not the marathon they were conducting). As he chomped on tubers and strange Australian fruits, he thought about Dave, his favorite local barista who was always quick with a latte and pain au chocolat, or Caprice at Dunkin' Donuts who started pouring his medium hot black coffee as soon as he walked in the door and never complained as he took his time picking out a few donuts to "hold him over till lunch."

At some point a kind of closed congress was held between Joel and some of the more senior members of the animal contingent. Custerd and the rabbits watched the discussion from a respectful distance.

After what must have been at least ninety seconds of watching and waiting, Custerd couldn't hold it in anymore. "Whaddya think they're talking about?" he bawled.

"Um, yeah, I was wondering the same thing," added Mr. Rabbit, rubbing his furry cheek with one paw.

"Us, presumably," said Benny, staring unblinkingly at the congregated animals.

"Of course, you old hopper! But *what* about us?" Custerd could no longer sit still and was up doing light stretches and twists of his torso. Mr. Rabbit was duly inspired and got up and started on some stretches of his own. It was a good idea to stretch before and after a long day of hopping and walking.

"I haven't the foggiest," said Benny the Bunny.

Joel and the animals talked for over an hour before reaching some sort of conclusion. Finally, Joel hopped a little ways toward the other wawas and gave them a beckoning wave. When they'd dusted themselves off and made their way over there, they were confronted with the following proposition:

"It's like this," started Joel. "We've been going some ways all together. But I've been talking with these fine animals and we all agree, if you're going to have a shot at finding this Rogo, you're going to have to split up."

"Split up?" asked Benny, his eyes going a bit wide.

"Yeah! Whaddya mean, split up?" Custerd reinforced. Sometimes Benny could use a bit of reinforcement, Custerd thought.

"No, no, don't get me wrong," Joel replied. "It's nothing like that. Nothing permanent. But you can only go so far in a hop-about all together. At some point, you have got to hop yourself more or less alone. BUT not completely alone, we're thinking. And not for too long either. We all think it might help if you were to venture out for a day or so and see what you might find separately. I'll stay with this lot here and we'll await your return."

"Um, so we're supposed to hop off into the forest by ourselves?" asked Mr. Rabbit, having a hard time understanding why it would ever make sense for him to purposefully go off anywhere without Benny the Bunny if Benny the Bunny weren't otherwise occupied.

"Not exactly," replied the leader of the koalas, the one who had first entered the light of their camp last night. "We think it would be best if you each went with an animal guide. You see, that's generally part of a hop-about—connecting with the animals, or at least the animal spirits you find out in the wild. But you've obviously already found a great number of us. Most of our conversation has been spent discussing which of our ... *menagerie* we would recommend you each journey together with. If you would be willing to trust us, we believe that we have found excellent matches for your individual sojourns."

And so it was that Custerd found himself heading out into the woods without the other wawas, accompanied by a young gray koala named Hank, just barely out of his adolescence.

Hank seemed to be a good sport. Custerd struck up some light conversation with him, mostly concerning the best breakfast spots in Boca, at which Hank nodded agreeably. But as he plunged into the forest without Mr. Rabbit and especially Benny the Bunny around, it got harder and harder for Custerd to maintain focus. He just kept thinking about how sore his paws were and how long it had been since he'd had a proper bath or a proper hot fudge sundae ... with fresh whipped cream, of course ... and nuts too—walnuts, preferably ... a cherry to seal the deal ... perhaps the whole thing would make better sense as a banana split when you really thought about it; that way you wouldn't have to make hard choices between ice cream flavors ...

Custerd started to slow his pace. Then he started taking frequent small breaks to "shake the lactic acid out." Then finally he just stopped. "Hank!" he cried. "I think I need a real break."

"Oh, thank god," said Hank. "Us koalas are not really made for all this walking."

"Us orange cats neither," said Custerd. "Say, what do koalas like to do?"

"Well, we very much like trees. Especially for sleeping and resting. Foraging is another big activity. When it's hot, we like to find some cooler bark to lie against. Sometimes we just like to hang a bit from tree limbs. But *most of all* we like eating eucalyptus leaves."

"Eucalyptus leaves, huh. What's that like?" asked Custerd.

"There's actually a good eucalyptus tree right over there." Hank pointed to a tall sturdy-looking tree with many high branches. "Would you want to try some? We'd have to climb up that tree a bit."

"Hank! You're a genius," Custerd exclaimed. Hank looked a bit abashed, not knowing why he was worthy of such a designation; truthfully, he really only wanted a snack.

"Orange cats are excellent climbers AND ... are you listening?"

Hank nodded vigorously.

"If we climb up that tree, we'll see the whole valley. We'll be able to scout the whole thing out. We'll see way more than just walking around. This is what I'm always saying ... work smarter, not harder ... you know, there's a real strain of Puritanism in this country, but ... well, not this country, I mean the country I'm from ... well, maybe— maybe Puritanism? You've got Puritans or pilgrims or that sort here, Hank?"

Hank shook his head and shrugged his shoulders, not following Custerd past the idea that he might get some eucalyptus soon.

"It's a whole thing, Hank, a *whole* thing. The long and short of it is ... we've got to get up that tree. We've got to get some of those leaves, and we've just absolutely got to get our backs up against some of that cool bark, so whaddya say, Hank?"

And soon that's indeed what happened. Hank led the way, and Custerd followed ably enough, being quite a good climber and, of course, naturally lithe of movement. It took a bit of effort to get to the top and a few moments for Custerd to huff and puff himself back into a normal rhythm of breath.

He joined in with Hank, chomping on some eucalyptus, both scrounging their backs into comfortable cool crooks of bark. The valley below was truly quite a marvel. The river they'd camped at cut through thick vegetation until Custerd was able to trace its line back to its source at a great waterfall coming down from an almost sheer cliff. And carved into a crack of that rocky cliff, Custerd thought he could make out a black shape, a dark hidden fortress of some sort. A bit ominous, perhaps, but Custerd didn't think about it too much.

Not at first.

Not until it was too late.

Instead, he thought the eucalyptus smell was pleasant enough, but in the end it was just another vegetable ... except ... except it did make him feel warm and pleasant where he wanted to feel warm and pleasant, all through his tummy and down into his toes. And his back felt oh so nice and cool. And the breeze was nice up so high. Hank was already asleep ... and who wouldn't want to sleep up in a lovely tree with puffy white clouds all around and such a nice feeling all over? In fact, it was the responsible thing to do, wasn't it? To go with his feelings, perhaps he'd dream of something important, something about Rogo.

But he didn't dream of Rogo.

He only dreamed of a blackness, sweating and twitching uncomfortably … he dreamed of a kind of hole … like the world was a bathtub full of beautiful sparkling water and sweetly calling birds and life of all sorts and joy and chocolate and love … but there was this absence too, this black fortress like a plug in the bath just waiting to be pulled and all would suck to nothingness, an empty blankness where no matter how loud he called … no one would ever answer.

***

From the beginning, Mr. Rabbit knew that he and Marvin the wombat would be fast friends. Marvin reminded Mr. Rabbit very much of Malcolm the Cairn Terrier. They had the same kind of stout, short-limbed bodies. The same sort of four-legged waddle when moving at less than a canter. But a clear power too. Like they were holding back their energy for the right moment to burst forth in dazzling displays of speed and athleticism.

There were differences too. Marvin's face was a bit flatter, his fur spiking out in all directions around his head, almost hiding his little ears, which were much smaller than Malcolm's. Malcolm's fur was a true golden, but Marvin's was mostly gray, although there was a touch of straw color in there too.

Also, Marvin had a certain gift of gab that Malcolm lacked. From the start of their journey together, they had fallen into all sorts of pleasing topics.

"Um," Mr. Rabbit had said as they made their way along the river at which they had camped the night before. "Benny the Bunny is a really cool guy. He's my best friend in the whole world. And Custerd is really great too. I just met him a few weeks ago and already we've gone on this great adventure together. Did you get the chance to meet them?"

"Yeah!" said Marvin. "Yeah, I just talked with Benny the Bunny a little bit. He said that you were his best friend too and that he'd appreciate it if I looked after you really careful like. And then Custerd came over and gave me a slap on the back and said something like, 'Hey! Take a little bit of this chocolate in case you and Mr. Rabbit get lost and need something to eat. But don't tell him I gave it to you because then it'll impress him that I did it anonymously. But then, of course, he'll know it was me because who else would have chocolate? You think he'll know it was me, right? Well, maybe tell him it was me, but tell him like I didn't want him to know; you get the picture, right? Anyways ...' and then kind of on like that for a really long time, and somehow at the end of it, I wound up massaging his feet for a little while and scratching his back."

"Huh, yeah, that sounds like Custerd," said Mr. Rabbit. "Well, that was nice of him to give us a little chocolate. Chocolate's very important to Custerd."

As they kept on hopping and walking, the forest began to get more and more dense. Mr. Rabbit was very glad that they had chosen to go along the river, where at least they could retrace their steps if they got lost.

"Say," asked Mr. Rabbit, "who's your best friend, Marvin?"

There was a bit of a pause where Marvin looked a bit contemplative, but then he soon brightened.

"Oh, I'm very good friends with Hank the koala, who's out with Custerd on his *so-churn*. And Jessie, of course—she's the beautiful kangaroo accompanying Benny the Bunny. She helped rescue me when the fire came through my part of the forest. She's a very fast hopper and was nice enough to let me ride in her pouch after I got all tired and worn down from running."

Mr. Rabbit and Marvin kept going for a little while in silence together, but it was a nice comfortable silence. The kind of silence that only good friends can enjoy, both knowing that the other is thinking pleasant little thoughts that they might share with each other soon but that need a little time to grow and blossom in the mind.

And as they walked on, the forest got denser and denser, and darker and darker, and cooler and cooler, as if somewhere up ahead was a great ice machine, chilling the land.

"Say," asked Marvin, noticing that Mr. Rabbit seemed to be blinking his eyes for extended periods of time and that he'd stopped hopping and was now waddling from side to side on his big furry feet. "You've been journeying for such a long time, you must be very tired. Would you like to ride on my back for a little while?"

"Well, I would not want to impose," said Mr. Rabbit, rubbing at his drooping ears a bit. "And normally I'm very enthusiastic on expeditions. But I have gotten to be a bit heavy in the eyes and sore in the feet and sort of stretched all over."

So it was decided, and Mr. Rabbit hopped up onto Marvin's back, and Marvin waddled along at his steady pace. At first, Mr. Rabbit rode on top of Marvin like a rider on a horse, with his lovely feet splayed out to each side and his front paws buried in Marvin's fur. It made Mr. Rabbit think of his time riding Felix the dog in Riverside Park. Only then he'd been holding on for dear life and the world had whipped past him in an indecipherable blur. Now the world sort of puttered along, and he could take a nice gander at the trees and the flowers and the buzzing insects and the little ripples in the river water.

After a while, even riding on top of Marvin became tiring. With Marvin's permission, he flipped over on his back, so that he was riding on top of Marvin, back to back. He looked upwards through the lightly swaying trees, up, up, up all the way to the jaunty, shuffling white puffs of cloud. And he became very, very sleepy. He rubbed his furry feet together and shuffled his back against Marvin's soft fur and soon fell asleep for a nap.

Marvin could feel the steady, deep breaths of Mr. Rabbit against his back. He barely weighed anything at all; it was no difficulty carrying him. Marvin felt warm in his heart to have made such a nice friend. Mr. Rabbit reminded him of his younger brother Marten. They'd not been like other wombat brothers. They'd hardly ever fought. Just played at racing one another through the underbrush or at who could dig the fastest. And Marten would burrow himself together with Marvin at night in their little hole under a small slumped tree that provided shade in sun and shelter in rain. Sometimes when it rained, the water would gather along the leaves of the tree and drop off them at a steady pace. It had always looked to Marvin like the tree was crying. And it had made him very sad to think that. And though it was a little sad, it had been a good tree. And Marten had been a good brother.

But the fire had taken the tree. And it had taken Marten too. And while Marvin could never go back to those old times or even the way he had been or felt in those days, Mr. Rabbit reminded Marvin of all the good that was still in the world.

***

It's hard to say what would have happened had Benny and Jessie followed directions.

But then they would have had to have been some other wawa and some other kangaroo. As it was, they were exactly who they were, so if you think about it, there really could not have been any other outcome. From the circumstances of their emergence in this world, from what was ingrained from the first to the gravitational pull of their friends and family to a thousand tiny details of their lives—all of this could only have produced the Benny and Jessie that had solemnly shaken paws that dark but still-warm night in the camp, looked into each other's eyes (Benny noticing amongst her generally tan fur a distinctive streak of white on Jessie's left cheek), and known immediately they were thinking the same exact thought.

So when Mr. Rabbit and Marvin had set off, instead of going their own way like they were supposed to—like Custerd and Hank had done—they had snuck behind the small wawa and his new wombat friend. They kept a safe distance, so as not to be heard, but so that they rarely lost sight of the adventurers. And with Mr. Rabbit and Marvin following the course of the river, they largely succeeded in their mission. (Except for a few dicey moments when Benny the Bunny had fallen into a thorn bush and had to be excised by a heave ho from Jessie, after which Benny had been forced to pick innumerable thorns from his fur on the go as they'd raced to catch up with the young wawa and wombat.)

They saw the pleasant little chats the two new friends exchanged (although they couldn't hear). They saw Mr. Rabbit grow tired and start to take a ride on Marvin's back (and taking a page out of that book, Benny the Bunny took a rest by riding along with Jessie in her pouch, his wise head poking out, his beautiful black eyes sparkling with attention, his ears turned to hear all that buzzed and called and moved in the forest). And they saw Mr. Rabbit fall asleep and Marvin walk on through the evening until it was quite dark outside and the forest had strangely become rather chill and more and more difficult to navigate, so close were the trees.

And then suddenly, a clearing. No trees, just a long stretch of grass. A great wall ahead. A cliff face that seemed to go straight up forever. A crack in that wall hiding something enormous and sharp and black. A fortress that appeared to be woven from midnight, so that even the starlight that shone above was blotted out by an ooze of darkness that seemed to emanate from it, as if the fortress were the opposite of the resplendent stars above; instead, it was a black star shining some kind of anti-light, a watching blackness piercing outwards, blacker even than the space between the stars. And everywhere that anti-light looked, there was the icy cold of fear and malice.

Benny the Bunny and Jessie watched from the forest as Marvin jostled Mr. Rabbit awake. They looked ahead toward the fortress. Faintly they could hear Mr. Rabbit say:

"Well, I agree. I don't like it at all either. But we're on a hop-about. We're looking for Rogo. He was Benny the Bunny's friend. And Benny the Bunny's my friend. I suppose we can't just not look because we're scared. Something tells me it's exactly when we're scared that we are most likely to find."

So Mr. Rabbit and Marvin walked toward the black steps that led up to the enormous black door of the fortress. A large human would have looked like an insect walking up those stairs. Mr. Rabbit was just a speck. But his back was straight, his eyes were clear, and his heart was true. Though sometimes in this world, that isn't nearly enough.

"We can't let them go in there alone!" cried Jessie, her eyes wide with panic. Benny the Bunny shook the astonishment of seeing the enormous black fortress from his head.

"Of course! Let's go!'

They hopped as fast as they could. But something in their hearts told them to keep hidden and to move along the wall of the cliff's crack, so as they reached the stairs and poked their heads around to look up toward the door, the man who opened the door to greet Mr. Rabbit and Marvin with pale, outstretched arms didn't see them looking up at him with wary eyes.

"Go back. Warn the others," whispered Benny.

"Never," Jessie whispered in harsh shock.

"This isn't a question of bravery," Benny whispered again. "I'm small enough. I can perhaps sneak in unnoticed. And you are fast enough. You can get back to the camp far quicker than me. If we do not return, you and the others will need to come for us."

Whipsaw across Jessie's face came anger and hurt and fear and then finally acceptance. She nodded and quickly pressed her right front paw to Benny's right front paw. She hopped away, being careful not to make any loud noises. As Jessie left, Benny began pressing himself to the wall and started sneaking up the black steps, his paws gliding silently along, his long straight ears twitching with concentration.

Up ahead he saw the back of the man leading Mr. Rabbit and Marvin into the open door, Mr. Rabbit nodding politely at something the man was saying. Benny continued to sneak—quick, quick now—with all the pace he could muster while keeping himself pressed against the wall.

The man entered the fortress, first beckoning to Mr. Rabbit and Marvin to join him. Marvin gave one last look outside before hustling after Mr. Rabbit. Then the door began to close, letting out a loud yawning noise.

There was a moment of hesitation as Benny's rational brain tried to formulate a plan but began to panic as it realized there was no time. And so another part of Benny took over, this one driven by instinct and intuition and most of all, love for Mr. Rabbit.

He bolted. Fast as he could for the closing crack in the great door. His straight ears whipped back, his eyes tearing in the wind, but with all of his speed, he wasn't going to make it. With all of its weight, the door was closing too fast.

Stubbornly he focused all of his might on that almost-gone crack in the doorway. His breath stopped. His vision blotted out. His muscles seemed to tear out into some new gear. Faintly, there was the memory of his hours running in the park, like the thoughts of some ghost he passed through and, unbidden, felt. But there was a stubborn pride in those distant feelings ... he would run full force into the already closed door if he had to ...

... and with one last aching stride he slammed into it. Into the wedge of the doorframe and the crashing door. Slammed together at once between them, and somehow ... somehow squeaking through to the other side.

He landed in darkness. And thankfully, with his soft fur and fluff, in silence.

For several rapid beats of his heart he lay there, letting his eyes adjust to the blackness around him.

Up ahead was a globe of sickly yellow light. A man held some kind of electric torch on a long staff. Mr. Rabbit and Marvin were in that globe of light, waddling after the man. And something else too. Something Benny hadn't noticed before while watching his companions from afar. A wawa walked with them too.

A large gray koala wawa, probably three times the height of Benny the Bunny and vastly wider too. He was worn—even more worn in areas than Benny himself. He must have been a very old wawa indeed. And while he smiled widely enough, there was a stiffness to his walk, an awkwardness to his movements. There was something not quite right about him. Not quite right at all, Benny the Bunny thought.

Benny moved in the shadows. He thought of Custerd and the hours he had spent watching his agile movements when they were still young, and he did his best to emulate that great orange cat. So Benny slinked along in the shadows, following the globe of yellow light.

The man's back was to him, but he could hear his voice—deep and lazy sounding, as if he were barely making the effort to form the words. As if he were lulling himself to sleep. Soft, but something false to the softness, like a great ball of cotton enveloping a tiny razor-sharp knife.

The man said:

"By all the tears in heaven ... this place? What is *this* place? Why, Mr. Rabbit, this place is *knowledge*. What else could it be? When the sirens sing, Mr. Rabbit, do they not always sing of truth, of *revelation*, of *knowledge*? The lie is that we cannot follow their song. That's the *lie*. Come, let me show you what I have found here on the edge of things. I think you will find much that will help in your search, help you in your finding. Here, dare I say, we are all found."

Then the man turned his head, so Benny saw his sharp nose in profile and his high forehead but not much else. He was looking down at Marvin, and a flash of violent irritation seemed to wholly possess his features, then soften into a slyness.

"Except … except what I'd like to show you … to help with your searching. Your wombat friend will have to stay behind. Only humans and wawas in the next room, I'm afraid. There is a … sanitation issue."

Benny could see Mr. Rabbit scrunch his brows down. "Oh, but I'm no cleaner than Marvin."

"Yes, yes, I *am* afraid the rule is *quite* firm. But no worries, there is an … auditorium. Virgil, would you please take the young wombat through the side door into the viewing area."

The stiff, awkwardly moving koala wawa, apparently named Virgil, nodded mechanically at the man and gestured to Marvin. There was a whimpering look of desperation in the way Marvin looked at Mr. Rabbit as he shook his head from side to side. Mr. Rabbit looked utterly puzzled. Too late he said, "Well, maybe I should go with Marvin, then." But Virgil was already leading the wombat reluctantly away, and the man subtly put his body between Mr. Rabbit and Marvin.

"Marvin! Marvin, is that his name? Oh, come now." The man opened the door in front of him, gesticulating at Mr. Rabbit to go ahead. "All shall be *revealed*, my new friend." Through the doorframe there was only another dark room. But something in the air of the room, a kind of hollow wideness to it, made clear to Benny that the room was a vast space, with ceilings unspeakably high above.

Mr. Rabbit hesitantly moved into the room, his head hanging in confusion and worry. The man let the door slowly creak closed on its own as he himself entered the room, so it was relatively easy for Benny to silently sneak inside and press himself to the interior wall on the opposite side of the door to the one by which the man fiddled with something unseen. Meanwhile, the man kept up his speech.

"Up ahead, Mr. Rabbit. A chair for you. Just trying to find the light. We have got electricity in here. One of the few places in this old palace."

Mr. Rabbit followed the man's gesturing and was soon lost in the dark outside the globe of the man's glowing staff. Benny could hear the slight swishing as Mr. Rabbit felt his way ahead with no light to guide him. The man was so huddled to his task against the wall, Benny could still not make out his features. Still he talked in that rhythmic, false softness.

"Marvin, Marvin, Marvin. You know, Mr. Rabbit, that brings up a very interesting point. Very few bother to study wawas. But *I* am an exception. Maybe *the* exception. So I am perhaps the rare creature who knows that while men and animals cannot comprehend each other in speech, wawas, being ... perhaps ... something *in-between* ... can often understand and speak with both. So while he's just another wombat to me, no different than any other, to *you*—to you, he is Marvin. Isn't that extraordinary? Something certainly to be studied—*examined*, even."

Benny could hear Mr. Rabbit bump up against something in the dark—the chair, presumably—and begin to climb onto it and sit down.

"You know, Mr. Rabbit. I heard it said once of animals, like your friend Marvin, that they could see God in the world. See his work and his magicks and his spirit explicitly. You see, animals act on instinct, without *moral* choice. We humans—well, God has hidden himself from us so that we may choose freely. For if we saw him in the world, there could be no choice of right or wrong. Doesn't seem quite fair, does it? Especially when he *Himself* has so much to answer for, hmmm? Tell me, Mr. Rabbit—as a wawa, as something *in-between* ... do you see God in the world?"

With that, the man finally flipped the switches he was fiddling with and a number of things happened very rapidly.

The light was everywhere, blinding. As bright and clinical as a hospital operating room. And, like some old nineteenth-century operating theater, there was an audience. To each side of the door they had entered by were walls of boxes with clear plexiglass walls facing into the room and cold metallic walls in every other direction. Some were empty, but the rest, Benny could see in a flash, were filled with wawas of all sorts—bears and frogs and koalas and cats and dogs and rabbits. Many were pressed against the clear wall watching the proceedings, any noise they might make utterly silenced. Others were more resigned and sat slumped somewhere in their box.

In one box was Marvin the wombat, and seeing his friend Mr. Rabbit sitting on a chair in the middle of the room, he threw himself against the clear plexiglass wall with all his might, snarling and clawing at it to no avail.

For he must have seen what Benny now watched in what seemed like slow motion. The catch holding a large circular cage to the high ceiling had been let go, and it was falling toward the chair in which Mr. Rabbit sat.

And as Benny the Bunny saw the cage begin its fall, he caught clear sight of the man for the first time.

But he wasn't merely a man.

He was naked from the waist up except for a large gray fur worn down his back. His hair, though thinned away in the front, was unkempt, wild, and long. He was pale as porcelain except for his cheeks, which were red as blood. And he smiled to watch the cage fall. His teeth bared. They were not as a man's teeth—his canines long and flashing like daggers. And Benny knew instantly whom he saw: The Wolf.

Not a single further thought passed through Benny's mind. He was surrounded by light, but already his mind was taken into the blackness. He moved without even knowing it.

He ran.

Pure motion. Pure speed. He moved on instinct. A singular goal that had no time to even announce itself.

He ran like he had never run before. Not even as he had run earlier to catch the fortress's door. That was Benny running as fast as Benny could. This was something else. Something within himself running; some deeper part of Benny that took over, the part of Benny that was the most *Benny* of all the parts that made him up.

In less than a breath he was to the chair with the cage descending overhead. So fast was Benny, the cage seemed like a softly falling snowflake. He gathered up Mr. Rabbit in his arms, their soft fur pressing together.

He ran.

The cage fell all around them.

There was no contest, though. Benny hopped with great bounding leaps of speed, Mr. Rabbit's face tucked into his shoulder, his arms and great furry feet wrapping around Benny in a tight hug.

CRASH!

The cage had fallen. But the sound was as something distant and meaningless. Benny was past the cage and on to the edge of the great room. And without picking one way or another, he was through a door into blackness again and down halls, bouncing off the walls in the dark, passing through more doorways, entrances, and exits, and farther and farther, and faster and faster, and the black world grew blacker until there was nothing but darkness.

Benny slowed.

And he stopped.

In his mind, Benny saw a vividly heightened vision of The Wolf, growling, slobbering, yellow teeth sharpened to points, howling out after them, his eyes full of some demon.

Does The Wolf follow?

It seemed as if they were in pure blackness now. As if they were somehow *nowhere.* Just blackness on and on in every direction.

Benny tried desperately to control his breathing and hunkered down in the pure dark, Mr. Rabbit still clutched in his arms, their hearts beating against each other like hummingbird wings.

THE GREAT CUSTERD CAPER

First light had turned the sky from black to midnight blue, yet the stars still soldiered on. Opening his eyes high up in the eucalyptus tree, it seemed to Custerd as if some sorcerer had cast a spell on the world. Beautiful dark, dark blue and bright white pinholes of light and not a tree or cloud between him and the great dome of the sky. Quite a thing to see too after the blackness of his receding nightmare; in fact, he felt as if he had walked from one dream into the next. Only maybe it was more than a dream; maybe it was a glimpse of the true world that always surrounded but could never be seen or touched. It felt like maybe he could walk right off his tree branch and into the sky and far away from here, like he could float and watch it all from afar. Escape. A great pair of eyes in the sky. Benevolent and kind, but removed. Not part of the drama anymore.

Soon, though, the ethereal elixir of first light broke with the garish reds, oranges, and yellows of sunrise. Custerd felt a kind of shrinking, like he had receded within himself. Gone from having touched some sacred space within to having become plain old Custerd again. He remembered himself. He remembered he loved reds and oranges and yellows, especially when they were big, bold, and, yes—garish.

Custerd remembered and Custerd knew: higher truths, the firmament of dreams, and grand unseen mysteries—these things were important—but plain old Custerd was important too.

He knew something else as well. He knew, sure as he knew he loved chocolate, that there was a reason he couldn't float away. Somehow he knew:

His friends were in trouble.

And he was the only one who could save them.

***

When Custerd and Hank the koala had made their way back to camp, the animals had been stirred up into a riotous commotion. Custerd pushed his way through until he got to the center of the hullabaloo. There, Jessie the kangaroo was telling Joel and the elder animals about the danger Mr. Rabbit, Marvin, and Benny the Bunny were in.

"... and so I hopped back fast as I could to tell everyone. That man ... there was just something awful about that man. Like the blackness of that terrible castle had seeped into his soul."

"Jessie!" Custerd cried. The whole crowd turned to face him. "I'm going to need you to start at the beginning." He shook his paws downward as if telling everyone to settle. "Please, I'm already formulating a plan. Would this old cat lead you astray? I just need the details. Jessie, please go on."

So Jessie told her tale of the unknowable dangers Marvin and the wawas faced in that black castle. Custerd listened intently, nodding along. As he listened, worry entered his heart, but some strength within him kept it at bay, kept it from overwhelming his thoughts. Instead, his mind whirled with possibilities, with plans and strategies, razor-sharp tactics and counter-tactics of cascading complexity.

When Jessie had finished speaking, Custerd raised a paw in the air.

"OK, OK, I've got it. I'm going to need all of your help. But first I'm going to need a pair of scissors. I'm going to need something sticky, a sack of some sort, Joel's didgeridoo, and I'm going to need one of you kangaroos or wallabies to donate a wee bit of fur. Now, who's ready to get crackin'?"

"I've got the didgeridoo *and* the scissors," yelled Joel with enthusiasm, and a whoop of excitement went into the air that someone had taken charge, that there was confidence and a plan. After those first moments of panic, any call to seemingly useful action was a welcome tonic.

Later, after a long walk, as the reality of the black fortress loomed ahead and, in the fullness of time, each had reflected upon the plan, doubt and fear sprung up in the hearts of wawa and animal alike, not sparing the usually bombastic orange cat in the least. Instead, as he began to take those last final steps before the point of no return, Custerd's head hung low as if the weight of his task physically pressed down upon him.

Then, alone, he entered the clearing before the black castle and his head swung up and his eyes gleamed with dancing fire.

The show had begun.

Custerd had entered the arena.

***

Benny's breathing finally settled to a rhythm only somewhat elevated above the norm. The blackness was still everywhere; he couldn't see his paw an inch in front of his face, but he could feel Mr. Rabbit. Feel his fur and warmth. They were out in the wild now, in the black between the stars, in the maw of The Wolf. It was as if the fortress itself was The Wolf and they had been sucked into its gullet, into its deepest depths.

But they were together.

"It sure is dark here," said Mr. Rabbit. A smile, invisible in the blackness, flitted across Benny's mouth. Mr. Rabbit was still Mr. Rabbit. And he was still Benny the Bunny.

"We're going to have to feel our way out," Benny replied.

"Um, how are we going to know which way is out and which way is further in?"

"We're going to feel for my paw-prints and retrace them."

"Oh. Oh, wow. That's a really good idea!" said Mr. Rabbit. "I'm not sure what I'd do without you."

"Without me, you wouldn't be stuck in the dark," said Benny.

"Oh, well, maybe, but I'd just be stuck somewhere else. I'd rather be stuck with you here to help me find my way back out again than stuck somewhere maybe with a bit more light but no Benny the Bunny to help me out."

Again the invisible smile came to Benny, and he put his arm around Mr. Rabbit's shoulder and gave him a squeeze.

"I'd rather be stuck with you too," said Benny. "I'd rather be stuck with you in the dark than free as a bird soaring in sunshine."

"My sentiments exactly," said Mr. Rabbit.

And so, holding hands so as not to lose each other in the blackness all around, Benny and Mr. Rabbit began feeling about with their feet for the ridges of Benny's paw-prints.

***

For the second time in only a few hours, a small figure ascended the wide black steps leading to the dark fortress carved from a crack in an impossibly high wall of stone, this one bright orange and entirely alone. Once again, the front gate opened. Once again, The Wolf appeared.

This is what he saw.

An orange wawa cat making his way up the stairs, having to lift himself up each step with his front paws as if he were climbing over a one-sided fence, and then once he had succeeded in hauling his considerable torso over the step, he would lie there huffing and puffing for what seemed like an increasing period of time with each subsequent step before summoning the energy to proceed to the next step and the next heave ho.

The orange cat appeared to have plastered yellow-orange fur to his head under his chin and encircling his head behind his triangular ears. The plastered fur, like an ersatz mane, continued down about a third of the cat's back, and there was also a puff of the fur covering the end of his rather worn-down tail. The Wolf supposed that the orange cat was attempting to appear to be a lion for some bizarre reason, perhaps some ploy having to do with the large sack he kept tossing up to the next step in front of him. Oh dear, such a misguided attempt at misdirection. Clearly the faux lion/orange cat had no idea with whom he dealt. But The Wolf would play along; oh yes, he quite enjoyed playing along.

"Why, hello!" The Wolf called out to the orange cat. "Now, who is this mighty lion I see approaching my lonely palace?"

"Ah shucks, hold on a minute, won't you!" Custerd yelled back, struggling to haul his sack and body up yet another enormous step. "Always keep your audience anticipating, that's the first rule," thought Custerd.

In his good time, Custerd got himself within spitting distance of The Wolf.

"OK, OK, here I am ... Now! Are you ready for the chance of a lifetime, sir?"

"I dare say I am," replied The Wolf with a smirk.

"My name is Ogor the Lion," continued Custerd. "A travelling merchant of much repute. Having grown bored with ruling the savannahs with an iron claw, I have chosen to spend my days bringing only the highest quality in fine silks, perfumes, and jewelry to, um ... rural country gentlemen like yourself. But *fear* not; my prices won't make you see *red*. No, no, no, my good man! Once king of the jungle, I am now king of the fire sale! What say you? Would you be so good as to let me show you my wares in the fastness of your lovely home?"

"Far more important, where indeed the magic trick lives or dies, is the second rule," thought Custerd. "Misdirection. Always keep them looking where you want, not where they think they should. Look at the lion, not the sack."

The Wolf opened his arms wide and smiled even wider.

"Well, of course, my fierce lion; how could I deny you entry with an offer such as that?"

"That's what I'm saying!" bawled Custerd, already pushing his way past The Wolf and through the entrance.

"Some folks just aren't so clever in the old thinker as you, my friend," Custerd added, knocking his free paw against his head while looking back at The Wolf as they both entered into the blackness of the fortress. Then, looking past The Wolf, Custerd stole one brief glance back at the closing door before charging even more rapidly forward.

"That's right, that's right. You know what, my new friend? I think we're two of a kind!" said Custerd.

"Oh, I dare say you are correct," replied The Wolf, stepping quickly behind his next prey. The last ones might have made a temporary getaway until Virgil assuredly rounded them up, but this one would not be nearly so lucky as to have even a momentary reprieve from his inevitable destiny.

***

Mr. Rabbit's big, fluffy, and very sensitive feet turned out to be very effective at finding Benny's paw-prints, and the two rabbits were soon on their way, feeling along in the dark back toward the room of horror that they had escaped not so very long ago.

As they slowly made their way in the dark, the two rabbits found themselves thinking about what they had seen in that room.

"Benny, did you see all those wawas locked away?" asked Mr. Rabbit in a whisper.

"I did. It was horrible," answered Benny.

"Why do you think they were locked away?"

"I'm not sure. I haven't yet had time to think it through."

The rabbits were quiet a moment except for the shuffling of their feet as they felt their way forward, trying to avoid stumbling into a wall or hole.

"We have to free them," said Mr. Rabbit.

"Yes … yes, we have to free them," said Benny.

A flinty resolve came into the eyes of both rabbits, although you couldn't see that in the dark. Those eyes saw nothing as well, but looked forward in determination nonetheless. Neither rabbit knew how they would manage to confront The Wolf, but they knew that together they had to find a way.

Mr. Rabbit thought of his friend's sure paw gripping his in the dark. If any rabbit in the wide world was wise enough to think of a way to rescue those wawas, it was Benny the Bunny.

Meanwhile, Benny still felt a stomach-dropping fear when he thought of The Wolf, remembering all the times that he'd dreamt of him before. Or dreamt of his many different faces. But he trusted that Mr. Rabbit's indomitable courage would steel him for when the time came. And he trusted that Jessie had made it back to the camp quickly and that help was on its way.

He thought again of Mr. Rabbit. Squeezed his paw as if to be sure he was really there—a light in all this dark pressing on Benny in every direction.

***

The room The Wolf led Custerd into was pitch black.

"Just ahead there, just ahead is a chair for you to rest on," said The Wolf.

Custerd began to proceed forward only to suddenly feel his sack wrenched from his hands. He let out a *yelp* of surprise.

"Of course, I'll have to hold on to this for safe-keeping. Wouldn't want any of those silks to tear or perfume bottles to shatter in the dark."

Custerd began to protest but was immediately silenced.

"No! No! No trouble at all, Ogor. Just as soon as I get this light on, I'll hand it back, lickety-split. Now off you go. Just ahead. That's right."

And, much like Mr. Rabbit before him, Custerd found himself without any protection, wandering forward in the dark, shuffling his feet along the ground, and holding his front paws out ahead of him, bracing to run into something. Indeed, before he knew it, he'd found a chair. The first chair he'd seen since he'd left Lisa and Jo at the Park Hyatt. It felt very nice to climb on up and take a load off. It had been a long, long walk since the Park Hyatt.

Thump! Blazing light ignited the room.

The sound of a catch releasing echoed high above.

Custerd's mouth hung open to see the immensity of the room, to see the row upon row of wawas pressed against their clear plexiglass cages, to see Marvin the wombat, aroused once more, slamming his body again and again against that plexiglass wall.

Such was his surprise, Custerd didn't move a muscle as the cage crashed all around him.

***

They had wandered along in the dark for a long time when the rabbits saw a hard white light flash on in the distance. A faint luminescence reached all the way to them, and they could just make out each other's faces for the first time in hours. They smiled to so suddenly see one another again. Then they were off, now at a much faster pace with the light out front to guide them.

As they moved forward, more and more was illuminated. They now moved down a cold industrial-seeming hallway, the walls made of something like brushed metal but colder and odder than any metal the rabbits were familiar with; it seemed almost alien, like the dead, fossilized skin of some unnatural infection. It gave the rabbits the shivers and they rushed ahead, not wanting to stay a moment longer than they needed.

Soon they skittered up to the small opening of light, slowing as they got close, but sliding a bit along what had become cold metallic ground. The last few feet they tiptoed, poking their heads as little as possible into the opening's light to look out at the vast room they had so desperately fled earlier.

Mr. Rabbit had to quickly bring both paws to his mouth to suppress an involuntary gasp at what he saw: Custerd sitting in the chair he himself had sat in not so long ago, surrounded on all sides by the circular cage that had almost trapped Mr. Rabbit if it hadn't been for Benny the Bunny.

The Wolf was pacing, almost seeming to lather from the mouth, shouting a deranged monologue.

"So clever, Ogor! So, so clever! But, I suppose, not clever enough. Or even *beginning* to take the very *first* step toward being *clever* enough. In the end, not so much a lion—just a *cat*. And judging by the wear marks on your ears and nose and especially on that dreadful tail of yours with that garishly gauche fur you've covered it with like a bad toupee, I would say a cat about eight lives through the allotted nine."

Just then, Mr. Rabbit felt something heavy and terribly hard squeezing his shoulder. He twisted himself about as he felt his feet leave the ground. He was suspended in air next to Benny, who found himself in the same predicament, staring into the vacant eyes of a large koala wawa.

Virgil had found them.

***

Custerd remained calmly seated while The Wolf ranted. The calmness in his demeanor seemed to only spur The Wolf on to greater levels of agitation, which was pleasing to Custerd in a way that he supposed he should feel guilty about. But he also supposed there was only so much personal growth one could expect at any given time. For now, he let himself enjoy the small pleasure he took in his captor's unhinged discomposure.

After a time, The Wolf seemed to be running out of steam. Custerd interjected:

"Say ... why wawas? What's the purpose?"

"Exactly!" The Wolf replied, regaining momentum. "What *is* the purpose of a wawa? And *how*? Have you ever even stopped to think for a second as to *how*? How is it that you're lying there as dull and dumb as any toy one minute, then Awake the next? And by what means? What magic powers your limbs? What mystic energies propel you forward? From what heights or depths are your thoughts conjured? I've studied and I've studied. And I've learned things far beyond what you could possibly dream, beyond the dreams of physics, even ... but that last taunting enigma ... that subtlest, unimagined force by which a wawa lives ... when I have seen that unseeable thing, when I *know* it, when I *pin* it, when I *bottle* it, when I *CONTROL* it ... then—then ..."

The Wolf trailed off, paused a moment. Slowed down. Seemed to hesitate, to take on a more thoughtful aspect.

He won't say the last part, Custerd thought, might not even realize the deep-down truth of it. But I know how that sentence ends: *then I'll feel* safe; *then, no matter what, they will have* no choice *but to love me.*

But there can be no love in domination, only in vulnerability. And there is no safety but through love. That was the paradox by which bees buzzed and souls grew, on which galaxies spun and all meaning lived.

And thinking those thoughts, it seemed to Custerd as if some great black veil had lifted, and through new eyes The Wolf seemed as one blinded, an overgrown child feeling his way in the dark.

But a rather dangerous child nonetheless, for any hesitation once again left The Wolf, and he continued.

"I do not enjoy the price we pay for knowledge. But it is utter *insanity* to *eschew* it. And if I am the only man with the conviction to pay that price, well, so be it."

The Wolf continued to pace the room, never taking his once again increasingly seething stare off Custerd for a moment. Custerd, in his turn, did not for a second let his own wander from The Wolf's blood-fired eyes. Much as he might desire to peek past him.

"The things I know. The things I've seen. That darkness I've walked. The insight I've plucked. The connections I've intuited. The confusion I've cleaved. And you ... you come to me with *this?*"

The Wolf swung Custerd's sack up in front of him, looking small and pathetic in the man's hand.

"What did you hope to sneak in here that could have possibly made a difference, hmmmm?"

The Wolf tore open the sack and began to toss the contents out onto the ground. As Custerd watched The Wolf's confusion at finding inside only Custerd's second- and third-favorite Hawaiian shirts and an explosion of various chocolate candy wrappers, he reflected on the third rule, the most important rule of all: *a trick may or may not work, but an illusion never fails. Because an illusion is not a matter of shifting the eyes to look left at a lion when they ought to have looked right at a sack. An illusion is the whole framework, the whole setup. It's the lure of fine perception, the hidden falseness of any conception of reality. It's trying to win a game you shouldn't have even started playing in the first place, trying to decipher a magic trick when you should be looking out for Hank the koala climbing over the top of your door and sticking Joel's didgeridoo in the gap when you think you've closed it, so that any and all manner of animal might wander inside.*

And in that last moment—he had really been so good up until now—Custerd couldn't resist finally looking over The Wolf's shoulder at Jessie rearing her body back on her tail. And though he knew he really shouldn't, and that this was something he would have to work on with his psychiatrist when the time came, Custerd couldn't help but smile as she kicked forward both of her unimaginably powerful hind legs into The Wolf's only now slightly turning, very startled body, sending him soaring clear across the room.

***

Virgil, still holding both rabbits suspended in the air, marched toward the old familiar hall where he went to throw the wawas in and out of their cages. Of course they made their cases, their pleas and arguments, but they were not for him to listen to. Only Master was to be listened to. And though Master's desires were passing strange to Virgil, who was he to question the wisdom of Master? Hadn't this place chosen him? And after all he had been through too. After all of the lacerations of Master's life. The leering faces and taunting voices Virgil could not protect him from. This place had chosen Master. This place of power. Chosen Virgil too, in a way, because Master had been chosen.

Still, it was oh so odd, all of these years. And all of his kind that must be ignored and kept.

But what were Virgil's thoughts compared to the thoughts of Master? And when, as if it were a game, Virgil was torn limb from limb, hadn't Master tried so desperately to stop it? Hadn't Master stooped, gathered him up, and sewn Virgil together again? Hadn't Master answered Virgil's doubts, saying, "My ways are not your ways. My laws are not your laws. Did I not pluck Virgil from black slumber? Where was Virgil when Master tamed this palace of unending nothing?"

And with these words echoing in his head, Virgil turned down the hall he knew so well, knowing immediately something was not right.

Surprisingly, the first thing Virgil noted was that all the cage doors were open. He thought, "That is not right. That is not proper. Master shall be oh so cross. Virgil has failed again."

The second thing Virgil noticed (which really ought to have been the first) was a fifty-pound rather irate wombat racing toward him at upwards of thirty miles per hour.

In the very moment Virgil registered the blur of fur and muscle moving toward him, he experienced a completely new sensation—he flew. Backwards and out of control. But still flying. Free for a moment.

It was the first time Virgil had something to smile at in he didn't know how long.

***

Mr. Rabbit stood back up from where Virgil had dropped him after taking Marvin's bull charge full force, briefly dusted himself off with his paws as he began to grasp the sudden turn of events, and realized that Benny the Bunny was also safely released from Virgil's grip and that Marvin was saying something rather frantically.

Mr. Rabbit gave him a big hug.

Marvin allowed himself a smile before beginning again: "We've got to go! No time! Hop on!"

So Mr. Rabbit and Benny did just that.

Marvin took off, running the opposite way now down that hallway. Mr. Rabbit saw empty cage after empty cage, and electric hope began to rise in his chest.

"STOP!"

Mr. Rabbit didn't think he had ever heard Benny the Bunny raise his voice quite that loud before. Marvin hit the brakes but still slid a few feet before coming to rest. Benny hopped off and raced toward one of the cages. Mr. Rabbit followed closely on his heels.

In one of the now-open cages sat an unmoving small gray wolf wawa. Running up and putting an arm on the wolf wawa's shoulder, Benny hurriedly exclaimed, "Come! We have to go!" The little wolf turned her head listlessly upward and merely looked blankly at Benny.

Mr. Rabbit presently arrived at Benny's side. After another couple of attempts to roust the little wolf, Mr. Rabbit tugged on Benny's arm.

"I think we're going to have to try to carry her."

Benny nodded.

The little wolf made no attempt to resist them as they, with some difficulty, each took an end and tottered out of the cage. Mr. Rabbit, bringing up the rear, could barely see anything, just a big smash of soft wolf fur in his eyes, trusting Benny to steer them to safety. His arms feeling heavy as anvils, they made it to the frantically anxious Marvin and made one last big push of effort to haul the little wolf up on top of the wombat. Wasting no time, Benny and Mr. Rabbit hopped up themselves, holding on tight to Marvin and their new companion as Marvin bolted once more down the hall.

***

A stream of animals and wawas were rapidly gathering in the great dilapidated front hall of the palace, now illuminated by the wide-open front door. Joel and Custerd (now freed from his cage by the combined lifting force of several kangaroos, wallabies, and koalas) were twin generals directing the flow of activity.

"I thought we were here to rescue two wawas and a wombat, not airlift the whole New Zealand Army," yelled Joel amongst the din of disorder and confusion.

"Where are they? We haven't much time. That man's coming for us soon," Custerd yelled back, but he was soon to his task again. "You two! Over there! That's right. OK, listen to this old cat; he's got the plan. Unless you're bigger than a joey, just find a pouch and hop in! Any pouch will do! No need to curate your selection! Let's go, people!"

Miraculously, the initially dazed wawas seemed to be getting the idea. A whole contingent of kangaroos and wallabies were loading their pouches up with the formerly imprisoned wawas. Even a few koalas were accepting some of the smaller wawas for a ride.

"Benny! Mr. Rabbit! Marvin!" Custerd cried, desperate to find his friends amongst the cacophony. Then somewhat more speculatively, "Rogo!"

He shook his head in frustration.

"Where are you? This is no time for dallying!"

In that moment, bursting from a side hallway came the charging Marvin with Benny, Mr. Rabbit, and a small wawa unknown to Custerd riding on his back.

"Hot dog, you rapscallion rabbits!" yelled Custerd. "I can't remember when I was so happy to see you!"

But the reunion was short lived, for in that moment The Wolf threw open the door to the hallway, looking like whatever mask of sanity he had worn before was entirely stripped away, waving a great saber in fury.

"AHHHHHH!" he screamed, seemingly beyond even forming words.

"Time to go!" yelled Jessie, picking up Custerd and putting him in her pouch. Marvin took off as well, and the whole army of animals and wawas fled out of the door of the black palace with The Wolf in hot pursuit.

Luckily, the wawas had largely made good time, and Joel, Jessie, Custerd, and Marvin with his riders were the last to flee out of the door. And The Wolf, running as furiously as he might, was no match for the speed of the kangaroos or the wombat. Still, he pursued them out of his palace into the bright light of day, running down his enormous steps with abandon.

Soon, wawas and animals alike had all made it to the grass and about halfway through the clearing when they heard an enormous crash.

About a quarter of the way down his great stairs, The Wolf had tripped and plummeted, falling hard and rough from step to step until finally settling with a loud thump on the bottommost black step.

Later, when they had time to reflect, Benny would hypothesize that if The Wolf had perhaps fallen that last step off the structure of the black palace and into the cool grass, maybe he too might have been saved. Maybe in the end, The Wolf was not really The Wolf of Benny's dreams but a mere reflection of the twisting influence of the darkness within that unholy fortress. Alas, they would never know. For fate did not grant The Wolf that one final fall, and he lay upon that bottommost step, screaming his rage out into the sky.

There was some more hope of redemption when Virgil appeared in the doorway of the palace. And indeed there was a moment when Virgil seemed to stand on a precipice of choosing to leave the palace as Benny and Mr. Rabbit beckoned and called to him. In the end, he, like The Wolf, only made it so far as the last step and merely watched the free wawas waving toward him with longing, then bent to help lift The Wolf back up to standing. In the end, Benny thought, our grace can prove just as great a trap as our flaws.

And so Benny watched, along with all of the other free wawas and animals, as Virgil, like a walking crutch, helped the broken man who had once been his bright, smiling boy ascend back up the stairs to the black palace.

***

Several days later, when Jo and Lisa met once again in the lobby of the Sydney Park Hyatt for a tea and to chat about their mutual adventures all about Australia and, most of all, to discuss their theories as to what the wawas were up to, they never dreamed that they would be confronted with the most raucous event ever to occur in the Sydney Park Hyatt's rather staid history.

A finely dressed waiter with beautiful posture was just setting down a three-tiered stand of sweets and little finger sandwiches on Jo and Lisa's table when a loud crash came from the front doors of the hotel. A slack-jawed waiter nearer the door had dropped a plate of many-colored macarons, so startled was he to see the scene that unfolded.

Jo and Lisa were even more shocked and found themselves floating up to standing, hands unconsciously rising to their mouths.

The wawas had returned.

Custerd, Benny, and Mr. Rabbit were all carried together in the pouch of the same kangaroo (who Jo and Lisa would later learn was named Jessie), while Joel did his best to keep up, hopping along beside them.

But they weren't the only ones. A whole stream of kangaroos and wallabies carrying various wawas in their pouches flowed into the lobby, overrunning the place—the kangaroos carrying either larger wawas or multiple smaller ones, the wallabies mostly keeping themselves to a single smaller wawa.

Jo and Lisa's faces lit up with pleasure, Lisa clapping her hands together once in excitement, Jo jumping up and down and all around.

"Mr. Rabbit! Benny! Custerd!" she cried.

Jessie hopped the three adventurers right up to Jo and Lisa, and the guys all crawled their way out and hopped down to the ground, Jessie helping Custerd out a bit with her paws when she saw him struggling to extract his pleasantly rounded torso from her pouch.

The guys ran into Jo and Lisa's arms, giving big warm hugs all around. Soon all of the wawas had departed their various marsupial conveyances, with effusive thanks, handshakes, and polite bows for the great service the animals had provided in bringing all the wawas back from the heart of the Down-Under Waste.

Benny, Mr. Rabbit, and mostly Custerd explained all that had happened to them to Lisa and Jo. The girls were greatly saddened to learn that despite having found and so bravely rescued a great number of wawas, they hadn't found Rogo, the lost wawa they'd set out to find.

At the mention of Rogo, Jo saw a very small and rather adorable wolf wawa shiver and shake a bit. The little wawa was very shy but seemed to immediately calm down when Jo picked her up and began to snuggle her. In fact, Mr. Rabbit and Benny were pleasantly surprised to see the very scared wolf they'd rescued, and who had been near catatonic for the entire journey back to Sydney, react positively to someone for the first time.

Lisa immediately took charge and began organizing the wawas into groups. After some solicitation and structured discussions, it was decided that a number of the wawas felt most comfortable returning with Joel to the Down-Under Club. Others expressed the desire to try to travel back to their various homes. Lisa, being an extraordinarily generous soul, promised to arrange and pay for the travel of any wawa that wanted to attempt the journey home.

Jo held onto the little wolf wawa, who never spoke throughout the discussion, but who shook and shivered whenever the word "home" was mentioned.

Seeing the way the little wolf took to Jo, Mr. Rabbit couldn't help but say, "Um, Jo, she seems to have taken quite a liking to you. I think there might be some special connection between you two."

"You know what, Mr. Rabbit," Jo replied. "I think you're right. If this little one is willing, I think I'll take her home with me. Maybe I can call her Erva, short for my favorite Roman goddess, Minerva."

As she said these things, Jo could feel the little wolf nodding her head in her arms. Then the wolf shifted her body back and forth until she poked her little head back out from Jo's body.

"I would like that very much," she said in a soft voice. Then, with a shake of her head, Erva indicated that she wanted to be set down, so Jo placed her on the ground.

Erva tentatively approached Mr. Rabbit and Benny.

"I'm sorry I've been so frightened," she began. "But it has been so long. And ..."

"You don't have to explain," said Benny, placing a comforting paw on Erva's shoulder.

"But I do have to explain one thing," Erva continued. "I've been trapped a long time. But this isn't the first time someone's escaped."

Silence spread out amongst the surrounding wawas like a shockwave.

"Many years ago, a small lion escaped when Virgil wasn't paying close enough attention bringing him and some other wawas down to ... to that man. The man was so horribly enraged. He made Virgil sleep in confinement like the rest of us for weeks. That lion, he was in the cell next to mine. I heard him say his name on a few occasions. It was Rogo."

Custerd swooped forward and went to his knees before Erva so that he could be on her eye level.

"Erva! Erva! Do you have any idea where he could have gone?"

"Pacing in his cell, he used to mutter all the time about where he'd go if he ever escaped."

"Where?" cried Custerd.

Erva took a big breath and let out an even bigger sigh. "He said he would go *home.*"

In the Woods

After a very long flight from Sydney to New York and seeing off Lisa and Jo (holding the still-shy Erva) and all of their other new wawa friends with hugs and smiles and tears, Benny, Custerd, and Mr. Rabbit took another flight.

This one rather short.

By the time that second flight had landed and they had found a car to drive them from Boston's Logan Airport out to the suburbs, the wawas were thoroughly exhausted from all of their travels. All buckled in the back of the taxicab, Custerd and Mr. Rabbit quickly fell asleep. Although no less exhausted, Benny the Bunny did not slumber. Instead, his tired eyes stared out of the window at the gray sky and the white snow falling everywhere. Though he could feel his mind working, he could not track down any specific thought. Only knew that it felt as though his brain were picking up some great weight and bearing it uphill. For what purpose, he could not say. He was only truly conscious of the gray-and-white images that flashed across his eyes through the window and then quickly disappeared, replaced by more gray and white. More bare tree limbs reaching into the sky. More softly swirling snowflakes.

He was going home.

No.

Not home anymore. Apartment 1K was home. Mr. Rabbit and Dr. Ursa and Pedro, and now Custerd too, were home.

He was going into the past. *It was always going to be this way.* He consciously registered the thought for the first time and felt it ring about, bouncing off the walls of his brain over and over again. *It was always going to be this way. It was always going to be this way. It was always going to end this way.*

The adventure was always going to end in the past.

True, the *looking*, the physical pursuit, was carried out over the length, depth, and breadth of the world. But the searching, the understanding, the revelation. That could only be found in memory, in the past. And the *finding*, that was a thing of unknowable subtlety, infinite fragility. A thing outside time and space. Benny knew that the finding, if indeed they were so lucky as to truly find, could only be a finding of the heart.

126

The taxicab dropped the wawas off on the corner of two sleepy streets, no other cars on the road at this time of night. Custerd gave a big yawn and Mr. Rabbit rubbed two furry paws against his eyes as he hopped out of the taxicab. Benny the Bunny stared at the old house. One by one, Custerd, then Mr. Rabbit joined him, standing on either side of Benny in the cold snow staring at the shingled roofs, the darkened windows.

In silence they walked around the house.

All the doors were locked. Every room empty of light or motion. The inside of the house seemed as cold as the outside. Void of life.

Once they had circled it completely, poking their heads into the windows and rapping at the doors with their paws, Mr. Rabbit was not sure what more could be done, but Custerd and Benny the Bunny looked out to the woods out back where the snow silently fell in the darkness between the trees.

"You don't suppose?" Custerd asked, his voice unusually reverent.

"It's the last place," said Benny, somehow knowing all along that this was their final destination.

So the wawas left the glow of the streetlights and the snow-covered landscaped yard and the stone walls and everything man made in the world.

They went into the woods out back.

They walked amongst the barren trees into darkness. Quiet everywhere. Stepping softly with their furry paws, hardly leaving a print on the icy crust of the snow.

Custerd and Benny walked without looking left or right. They knew their destination. And Mr. Rabbit followed, trusting his friends and the strength that flowed from their memories.

They walked at a steady pace, neither tarrying nor hurrying. They walked with seriousness, the self-conscious solemnity of pilgrims entering a holy land.

After some time, Mr. Rabbit could not say how long, they came to a depression in the ground. A hollowed-out area crowned with trees, their roots coming down the walls of the depression as if it were some great woven basket.

"This is where the ferns grow," said Benny the Bunny. Then he led them down the sides of the depression, hopping along a particularly large twisting root. Once down at the bottom of the depression, Benny put his paws to his mouth.

"ROGO!" he cried.

Custerd joined in. Then Mr. Rabbit.

"ROGO!" they yelled, their voices echoing out through the otherwise silent woods.

Nothing.

Custerd fell back onto his seat, sitting and staring forward at nothing, seeing nothing. Mr. Rabbit was surprised to see Benny also collapse into a seated position. So Mr. Rabbit sat down to join them. He placed his paw in Benny's paw, which, though limp at first, soon gave back a loving squeeze. Then Benny reached out and grasped Custerd's paw too. And they sat there for a long time, in the depression where the ferns used to grow as the snow fell all about them.

***

Behind a large root, in a hollowed-out and relatively warm spot, two eyes watched the wawas. Those eyes were wary and uncertain. But as they watched the friends sitting in silence for a long while, they decided they had watched long enough.

A small creature emerged from behind the root, his footsteps slow and halting. He looked worn and ragged. But he was still unmistakably the lion they had known.

Seeing him, Custerd shot up to standing, but he held himself back from running to Rogo, not wanting to frighten his old friend. Benny didn't move a muscle, but his eyes became very focused, as if they saw but one thing in all of the world. Mr. Rabbit felt a forceful stirring in his heart but tried to hold his emotions in as well, not wanting to intrude as a newcomer in an old drama.

Rogo walked slowly, ever so cautiously, over to the other wawas.

Then there was tentative hugging and there was whispered talking. Talk of a lot of things. About Australia. About The Wolf. About home.

Benny and Custerd asked Rogo if he would come home with them, if he would come in from the woods. But once you had been in the woods such a long time, it was not so easy to come in.

128

There was a special tree that grew right up against the house. In the cold of winter, its leaves had fled. And though the tree slept, it still dreamed dreams of warmth and sun and spring green and the thumping heart of the earth below. Rogo led the other wawas to the tree and they climbed up to the branch that stretched across two special windows. Windows that led into the two bedrooms of the little girl and the little boy that Custerd and Benny had grown up with.

They sat on the tree branch all together and looked into the blackness of those windows.

"Do you remember, Benny?" asked Custerd.

"Of course I do," Benny replied. "I remember it all. I remember playing all day. And I remember the days that were rather not playful too. But I always remember that after they got into bed, they would knock against the wall to each other. To say I love you."

"And we would too," said Custerd.

"And we would too," agreed Benny.

"When I came back home ..." began Rogo, but he soon stopped and silence weighed down on the four wawas. He gathered himself and began again.

"When I came back, everyone had gone. I didn't know what to do. So I waited. I waited and waited. I would come here to the tree and look in the window, but it was always dark.

"Then one day ... one day another little boy moved into the smaller bedroom. He was an only child. The bedroom that used to belong to my little boy was turned into a library. This new little boy, he had a small brown wawa bear named Gusto that he loved very much. Gusto was not Awake for many years, but after the boy loved him for a long time, he became Awake. And then Gusto would come to the window when he saw me on the branch and we would talk. He would ask advice and bring me cookies that the boy's mom had baked. And he told me it made the boy and him feel safe that I would climb up on the tree branch and protect them at night. But ...

"... but as they always do, the boy grew up and moved away."

Rogo paused a long while again.

"An older couple live here now. They're very nice. They drink coffee together in the morning at the kitchen table and have tea in the afternoons. They read under separate lamplights at night. The man always puts his out first. Sometimes the woman stays up very late, and I make sure nothing from out in the dark comes for them.

"The winter is always hard. They go someplace warm in the winter. I think they stay with one of their adult children in Florida or Georgia or some place like that. In the winter I'm alone."

"You know, you don't have to be anymore," said Custerd, much softer than Mr. Rabbit had ever heard him speak. "I've been alone ... thought I preferred it that way, even. But now that I'm going to stay with the whole gang in New York ... I feel ... I don't know ... I feel like I'm a part of something again. They said that I can sleep in the same room with them, that there's space for another bed. But I think I might sleep in one of the rooms in the second bedroom. There's space for two beds in there. When it's time for sleep, we can knock to them through the wall to say goodnight ... to say I love you."

The woods were a part of Rogo's mind now. He couldn't just let them go. His idea of home could not just turn in a moment. But Rogo thought about the possibility of change. About how love could transform things. How it had transformed the tree in which they sat from just a tree to something more. To something that hummed with the spark of love in it. You might not be able to say how exactly, but you could feel that spark in your soul when you climbed its branches or even just laid your paw against it. He thought about how his boy had loved him Awake. And how he'd seen Gusto loved Awake, watching almost like a second parent. He liked to think his love meant something to Gusto and to Gusto's boy. He thought about the couple that lived in his old home now, how at first he had had only bitterness in his heart for them because they had replaced what he loved. But the bitterness had drifted away. In the end, he had loved them too.

Rogo looked down the line of sitting wawas at Mr. Rabbit and his old friends Benny the Bunny and Custerd. He thought about all the years, how he had felt so abandoned, but he also thought about how they had searched halfway around the world for him.

The woods might go on living there in his mind, might live in his fears and in his dreams, but he was ready to come home at last. Rogo was ready to come in from the woods. He stretched his body forward, leaned out from the tree branch, and, for the last time, knocked on the boy's bedroom window.

And for the first time in years, Rogo heard the sound of his knocking returned. He heard Benny and Custerd knocking against the windows that had belonged to their boy and girl in the long ago.

SURPRISE

Spring had finally come again. The days had lengthened, layers of clothes had been stored away for another year, tentative smiles returned to the faces in the cafes and restaurants and in the streets. Spring had come and Mr. Rabbit was walking through Riverside Park again.

He was heading in the downtown direction, and when he passed the 91st Street Garden he tarried there, even though he was on a mission.

He didn't think Benny the Bunny would mind knowing that he'd stopped and smelled the new blossoming flowers. In fact, he rather thought he might encourage it, even if he had known the task Mr. Rabbit had set for himself. Benny the Bunny was, after all, a very wise bunny rabbit.

Dr. Ursa was busy with patients, but Mr. Rabbit had spoken to Custerd and Rogo about the idea, suggested that they might come with him, but they had had to beg off. Custerd had said, "Heck! You're not coming with *us*? Can't an orange cat get a chance to spend some time taking his little lion buddy to the Museum of Natural History? But if you do go, you better go today so as to catch Benny by surprise ... what? Of course we'll be back in time to eat the scones! What do you think this is?"

You see, Mr. Rabbit had been thinking a lot about how good a friend Benny the Bunny was to everyone. He was thinking that Benny the Bunny was always doing such nice things for him. Not to mention that he was always there to offer his wisdom whenever Mr. Rabbit got a bit confused or even, on rare occasion—befuddled. So Mr. Rabbit thought it would be a lovely thing to go down to Alice's Tea Cup, Benny and Mr. Rabbit's favorite breakfast spot (excepting The Rabbit Diner, of course), and pick up a great batch of scones for Benny and the gang to eat as a just a little thank you, a little surprise happy day present.

So Mr. Rabbit felt no need to rush himself as he sniffed along in the garden, finding beautiful early spring flowers of all sorts: the crocuses were in full bloom, the snowdrops on their way out but still holding on for a little while longer, and the daffodils just beginning to pop in great bursts of swaying color. It was a strange year with it having been fall, then winter (like usual), then suddenly blistering summer down in Australia, then once again back to winter. It was nice that things were back to their usual rhythm, that winter had dutifully thawed into spring without skipping ahead to summer or falling back to autumn.

After leaving the garden, Mr. Rabbit kept himself to an ambling pace. There were lots of dogs of all sorts out for walks. And there were children too, playing in the green spaces, kicking balls, and running and riding bikes. Mr. Rabbit liked to look at the flowering quince bushes as he walked and up above at the budding tree leaves everywhere and out at the sparkling Hudson River and New Jersey and all the vastness of America out there to his right.

Mr. Rabbit thought of his recent adventures as he went. He thought of all the faces of the animals and wawas that he'd met. He thought of Lisa and Jo and how it would be oh so nice for them all to get together at some point soon. He wanted to hear more of Jo's thoughts on outer space and time. He wanted to hear how Lisa was doing and if her travels had lightened her heart.

He was glad, though, to take this little walk by himself. He hadn't wanted to go to the Museum of Natural History without Benny there to remind him that he was perfectly safe and that all of the fangs and claws couldn't hurt him. Although he supposed he'd been to a far scarier place now. But still, it might be nice for Custerd and Rogo to have some time on their own to catch up on all of the years they had missed.

It was nice to have a little think on one's own, Mr. Rabbit thought. To turn over all that had happened while strolling along. It was strange how all those nights in the Down-Under Waste, when he was hungry and tired and full of doubt … it was strange how those all seemed so magical now that they were done and gone. Those moments, somewhere in the process of transforming themselves from amorphous, unrelenting reality into memory, they had taken on a weight and beauty that was impossible to see when he'd been living them. Now when he thought of those nights, he thought of the furry faces of Joel, Custerd, and Benny looking back at him from across the fire. He thought of those strange southern stars almost coming down to grab him. Almost like he could bathe his mind and soul in their otherworldly light.

He could have done without the scary parts. That was for sure.

Yet he supposed that the scary parts had their place. And who was he to say one way or another? You just had to take things as they came. He hadn't made the world—he hadn't made himself, even—so he just had to take it all as it was. Try to leave things a little better than you found them. That's about all you could do when it came down to it. Be brave. Trust in your heart. Trust in the hearts of your friends.

He could think those thoughts and know them to be true. Yet … yet he was still troubled. And not sure what to do with his trouble. It just sort of hovered there somewhere unspecific, somewhere between his stomach and the back of his mind.

When he thought of Dr. Ursa and Pedro and Custerd and The Rabbit Diner and his painting, and especially when he thought of Benny the Bunny, then that trouble seemed to sink away for a while.

But it was never really, truly, all the way gone.

Sometimes, unbidden, he would think of the darkness within the black fortress. And of the darkness within The Wolf. Perhaps more troubling than the darkness itself was the mystery of its origin. He and Benny had discussed those origins at length. Had developed conjectures and theories. But nothing satisfied. Understanding eluded them.

But that was OK. Benny had said, "Wounds take time and rest to heal. Understanding takes patience. We should always be patient with ourselves." And Benny the Bunny was very wise.

Before Mr. Rabbit knew it, he was already coming to the end of the downtown portion of his journey. So he had to leave the park and make his way east toward Alice's Tea Cup. And walking down the street, things were much the same as they had been in the park. Everyone was giving each other a bit of a break today. Smiling a little more. Rushing and shouting a little less. In their own ways, thanking the powers that be for the gift of a perfect spring day.

Soon Mr. Rabbit was hopping down off 73rd Street and into Alice's Tea Cup. All of his favorite employees were there. The one with the gorgeous curling black hair and easy smile, the one with the ever-concentrating face who was always focused fully on everyone enjoying their scones and tea, the one with the dramatic makeup who hustled all about pouring ice water for whoever might be thirsty.

The one with the beautiful black curling hair (whose name was Sofia) greeted Mr. Rabbit with her signature smile.

"Hello, Mr. Rabbit! What can I do you for today? Where's Benny the Bunny?"

"Oh, he's got a lot of little errands to take care of. But I'm actually trying to give him a bit of a surprise. I thought I'd come down and pick him up some of his favorite scones in the whole world. Also some for me—and Custerd and Rogo and Dr. Ursa, of course."

"How many scones in all are you thinking?"

"Um, let's see … hmmm, I guess two scones per wawa, so ten scones … actually, Custerd might be a little extra peckish—how about an even dozen, I think."

So Sofia showed Mr. Rabbit the day's scone menu. He picked out a half dozen mixed berry scones, since he knew those were Benny's favorite, four double chocolates so Custerd wouldn't be disappointed, and two pumpkin-flavored ones as a bit of a tasty curveball.

After he'd made his order, Sofia packaged up the scones and handed them over to Mr. Rabbit along with an ample portion of jam and cream to go on the scones and provide the necessary lubrication. But as Sofia handed over the package to Mr. Rabbit, a sudden fear came to him. He hadn't thought it through. The package was way too large for him to carry! Each scone alone was almost the size of Mr. Rabbit. He could never carry a full dozen on his own.

Seeing his distress, Sofia leaned over the counter and smiled once again.

"Say, Mr. Rabbit, these scones are pretty heavy for a stuffed rabbit to carry uptown. But I have to make a delivery not too far from where you live. Would you want me to come with you and I can help you carry yours?"

"Oh, thank you so much, Sofia!" Mr. Rabbit exclaimed. "I guess I hadn't really thought this surprise through all the way and was starting to realize I was in a real pickle. You're saving me!"

"Oh, it's nothing." Sofia smiled and threw her hand across the air as if to say the enormous favor was as empty as the air itself. "I'm delighted to have a friendly companion to chat with while I make my delivery."

So Sofia (carrying all of the scones) and Mr. Rabbit (only carrying cream and jam and still just about falling over) made their way uptown to Apartment 1K. They took a much more direct path than Mr. Rabbit had used on his way down, hopping on the subway at 72nd and Broadway.

When they got to Mr. Rabbit's building, he was a little surprised to see that Pedro wasn't at his post as usual. But Sofia offered to take Mr. Rabbit's keys and open the door to Apartment 1K for him; she even took Mr. Rabbit's scones, along with the whole rest of her delivery, up the stairs for him while Mr. Rabbit hopped along behind her.

As he got to the top of the stairs, he couldn't quite see inside the French doors because Sofia blocked his view, but he did feel a buzzing kind of energy coming in his direction. And then, once Sofia had swung open the French doors and stepped aside, he saw where the energy had come from. And heard a loud shout:

"SURPRISE!"

The living room of Apartment 1K was packed to the gills. Custerd and Rogo were there. (Custerd was even wearing his *first*-favorite Hawaiian shirt.) Dr. Ursa and Karen as well, both smiling and clapping next to a vase of fresh and friendly yellow-orange roses. Pedro was there, flashing that dazzling smile of his. John was there, holding Malcolm and Tuck, who both let out *ruffs* of joy. George from The Rabbit Diner was there, still dressed in his formal tailcoat and bearing a huge mouthwatering vat of *fraise mit schlag*. Jo, along with Erva and her parents, was there, smiling and waving. Lisa was there, looking elegant and a bit misty eyed. Joel, Hank, Marvin, and Jessie all the way from Australia were there, as were several of the wawas they'd rescued. Some of Mr. Rabbit's rabbit and groundhog friends from the local parks and even some from so far as central New Jersey were there. Sofia was there with her big smile and her big box of scones, which she was setting down and putting out for everyone to eat. There was tea and coffee already set out to drink too.

And moreover, covering every inch of the walls were Mr. Rabbit's paintings. It was the exhibit he had always dreamed of. There were his wild abstractions. His paintings of the parks and of the animals. His portraits of Dr. Ursa and Custerd. A whole little section of his portraits of Benny the Bunny and all their many varieties. And a big section of his recently completed paintings of their Australian adventure. Of all of the wawas of the Down-Under Club, of the stars and the land of the Down-Under Waste, of all the animals he had seen, of Custerd disguised as a lion. Even a painting of The Wolf, looking down, his face and body half covered in shadow, looking far more sad than scary.

And most of all, standing at the center of the room was Benny the Bunny, with a big smile on his little mouth and a sparkle in his beautiful black eyes.

Mr. Rabbit flew to him and they toppled over in a big warm furry embrace. "Thank you," he said, but for some reason it was hard to speak, and the words came out in barely a whisper. Then he and Benny stood up, arms around each other's shoulders, the whole room seeming to spin with smiling faces and clapping hands.

Mr. Rabbit found his voice.

"Thank you! Thank you, everyone! I don't know what to say. I'm so happy to see each and every one of you." And then after a brief pause he added, "I love you!"

Sometimes, and this was one of those times, Mr. Rabbit felt so full of love for all the creatures and flowers and things about him, it seemed love was bursting out of his tiny frame. It was hard to feel so much love. Hard to know what to do with it. And so easy to be hurt. So easy to be bruised by the world. So easy to look out and see the things happening that shouldn't and want to kill love, because love made the crimes of the world hurt that much more.

But despite it all, Mr. Rabbit never so much as considered shutting down his love or hiding it away. That was his great strength. And in those moments, like this moment right now, when love flowed through him with more force than a rushing rapid, he didn't break or fall or come apart. He let his heart dance with it all. He felt as though he danced at the edge of a pin in rushing wind and rain. He felt free and he felt beautiful. And he felt only love.

Manufactured by Amazon.ca
Bolton, ON

24924225R00081